You're invited to a

CREEPOVER ®

Will You Be My Friend?

written by P. J. Night

SIMON SPOTLIGHT

New York   London   Toronto   Sydney   New Delhi

This book is a work of fiction. Any references to historical events, real people, or real places are used fictitiously. Other names, characters, places, and events are products of the author's imagination, and any resemblance to actual events or places or persons, living or dead, is entirely coincidental.

SIMON SPOTLIGHT
An imprint of Simon & Schuster Children's Publishing Division
1230 Avenue of the Americas, New York, New York 10020
First Simon Spotlight paperback edition July 2015
Copyright © 2015 by Simon & Schuster, Inc.
All rights reserved, including the right of reproduction in whole or in part in any form.
SIMON SPOTLIGHT and colophon are registered trademarks of Simon & Schuster, Inc.
YOU'RE INVITED TO A CREEPOVER is a registered trademark of Simon & Schuster, Inc.
Text by Michael Teitelbaum
For information about special discounts for bulk purchases, please contact
Simon & Schuster Special Sales at 1-866-506-1949 or business@simonandschuster.com.
Manufactured in the United States of America 0615 OFF
10 9 8 7 6 5 4 3 2 1
ISBN 978-1-4424-9731-3
ISBN 978-1-4424-9732-0 (eBook)
Library of Congress Catalog Number 2014935635

CHAPTER 1

"Mom, where does this go?" shouted twelve-year-old Beth Picard. She gripped a large cardboard box in her arms and stood inside the empty hallway of her new house.

"What's it say on the top?" Beth's mom called back from the living room.

Beth glanced down at the box. "'Kitchen,'" she replied.

"I'll give you three guesses as to which room it belongs in," Beth's mom replied. "And the first two don't count!"

"Very funny, Mom," Beth said as she headed to the kitchen and placed the box on top of two other boxes, forming yet another cardboard tower growing out of the kitchen floor.

Beth and her mom were excited about moving into their new house. It had been built a few years ago and had only one set of previous owners. Even the paint on the walls still looked spotless. It felt like a fresh start for both of them.

Beth's mom had just started a new job. Beth was looking to make new friends and move on with her life, following . . . well, following whatever had come before—something she was not too clear about.

Beth hurried back out to the moving truck they had rented, climbed up the metal ramp, and grabbed another box. As she headed down the long front walkway, past hedges and flowering trees, she was about to call to her mom again. Instead she stopped just outside the front door and glanced down at the label on the top of the box. It said BETH'S BEDROOM.

Beth smiled as she walked into the house and headed up the stairs, proud of herself that she didn't have to ask her mom about every box she carried in.

Beth knew that her mom was a very organized person. At least that's what her mom liked to say about herself. She had told Beth that when she packed up their stuff at their old house, she made sure to group every box according to room. Then she made a label for each box to take the guesswork out of the unpacking process.

Beth took her mother's word for the fact that she was organized. In fact, Beth took her mom's word for just about everything. For reasons she didn't understand, Beth had trouble recalling the past. She searched her mind, trying to remember helping her mom pack up their old house, but could conjure no images of that or anything else from before. Beth couldn't even recall what their old house looked like.

More to wonder about, I guess, she thought as she stepped into her new bedroom and placed the box onto her bed.

Turning around, Beth caught a glimpse of herself in a full-length mirror leaning against a bedroom wall. Sunlight streaming through the window highlighted the spattering of freckles on her face. She shook her head, sending her shoulder-length auburn hair whipping back and forth.

As Beth was about to turn away and head back downstairs to grab another box, she caught another glimpse of herself in the mirror. In the glass she saw her reflection looking into another mirror, in which she saw herself looking into yet another mirror, and on and on, as if she were in a carnival fun house.

What? she thought, peering into the mirror at the multiple versions of herself. She leaned in closer and saw all the images of herself in the many mirrors lean in as well. She shook her hair again, and strands of copper-colored waves flowed back and forth in each mirror image.

Beth turned away and glanced back quickly, as if she was trying to catch herself, or trying to trick the mirror into going back to normal. Her mirror was still filled with multiple, endless images of herself, extending off into infinity.

Deep into the strange mirror, way off in the reflected distance, Beth could see the tiniest image. But it wasn't an image of Beth, and it wasn't moving as Beth moved. It was of someone in a long white coat. The woman appeared nervous, looking back over her shoulder again and again. Beth leaned in even closer to the mirror, so that her nose was touching the glass. And that's when the woman vanished from the reflection.

Beth had had enough. She didn't know if she was hallucinating or what, but it was time to get more boxes.

When she turned away from the mirror, all of the other Beths turned with her—all except one who stood still, staring straight out. Beth squeezed her eyes shut tightly, then threw them open quickly. The multiple images were finally gone. The single reflection of Beth, staring wide-eyed at herself in her bedroom, was all that remained.

She drew a deep breath and sighed.

"Beth!" her mother called up from the bottom of the stairs. "There's someone here to see you, honey."

I need some sleep, Beth thought, turning away and heading out of her room. Before she stepped out into the hallway, she whipped around quickly to make sure again that just one image filled the mirror. It did.

A few moments later Beth came face-to-face with a girl her age, standing on the front steps.

"Hi, I'm Chrissy Walters," said the girl. "I'm your neighbor. I just stopped by to welcome you to the neighborhood."

Beth smiled and said hi back.

Chrissy had short blond hair and two different-colored eyes—one blue and one hazel. Beth thought that was totally cool.

"I'm Beth Picard," said Beth. "And this is my mom."

"Nice to meet you," said Chrissy. "I've lived in the house next door for about six months. Your place has been empty all that time. I'm so glad you moved in, especially because we're the same age, I think."

"I just turned twelve yesterday," said Beth.

"Happy birthday!" said Chrissy. "I turned twelve a few weeks ago."

"Come into the kitchen, Chrissy," said Beth's mom. "We can't offer you anything but a glass of water, but you're welcome to sit on a packing crate."

Beth, her mom, and Chrissy all headed down the hall and into the large kitchen, where they found stacks of boxes, a few packing crates, and two glasses sitting on the counter.

"We haven't started unpacking the kitchen yet," explained Beth's mom. "Just a glass for Beth and a glass for me. Here, let me get you one." She popped open a cardboard box and unwrapped a water glass, then she filled all three glasses with water from the faucet.

"So you only moved into your house a few months ago?" Beth asked Chrissy.

"Yeah, I know a few kids from school, but it's nice to meet someone who lives just next door," said Chrissy.

"Where did you live before this?" Beth asked.

"California," replied Chrissy. "My mom's job moves us around a lot. How about you? Where did you live before this?"

"We lived . . . uh, we lived . . ." Beth stammered and then stopped short. She hit another brick wall in her memory. Try as she might, she could not come up with the name of the town she and her mom had just moved from.

"Rockport." Beth's mom jumped in. "About an hour from here. On the other side of the city."

"Oh, yeah, Rockport," Beth agreed, although the name of the town meant nothing to her.

"Did you forget where you're from?" Chrissy asked, tilting her head curiously.

"Beth was in an accident a few months ago, Chrissy," her mom explained. "Sometimes her memory is a bit fuzzy. But the doctors assured us that it will clear up with time. Right, honey?"

"Right," agreed Beth. "That's it. My accident." Though, in truth, Beth had no memory of having had an accident or seeing a doctor.

Beth's mom smiled at her and got up.

"Well, I'll leave you two girls to get to know each other better," she said. "I've got about a million boxes still to unpack. Nice to meet you, Chrissy."

"Nice to meet you, too, Ms. Picard," said Chrissy.

"So maybe we'll be in the same class at school," said Chrissy when Beth's mom had left the kitchen. "That would be fun."

"Actually, my mom is going to homeschool me," Beth explained. "She works the night shift doing medical research at the lab a few blocks from here four nights a week, but she teaches me before she leaves every evening."

"Oh," said Chrissy, unable to disguise the disappointment in her voice.

"But we could hang out together every day when you get home from school and on weekends," Beth added quickly.

Chrissy smiled. "That's great! So what kinda stuff do you like to do? I love reading, playing soccer, and watching movies."

"I like, um, all that stuff too!" Beth replied, not quite sure what she liked to do.

"But you must spend a lot of time alone," Chrissy

added. "Especially at night, with your mom working and all. Is she okay leaving you alone?"

"Actually, there's going to be a babysitter who stays here every night," Beth explained.

"Is she cool?" Chrissy asked.

"I don't know yet," said Beth. "My mom has to find someone now that we've moved. It's a little immature, I know, to have a babysitter at our age, but since my mom works overnight, she doesn't want me home alone all the time."

"That makes total sense," said Chrissy. "I just hope your babysitter is cool, for your sake."

"I'm sure she will be," said Beth. "My mom said I can help her choose the right babysitter. Anyway, I'm really glad you want to be my friend, Chrissy."

"Me too," said Chrissy. "I gotta get home now. But maybe we can hang out tomorrow."

"Great," said Beth.

Both girls headed outside.

"Bye!" said Beth, waving as Chrissy headed to her house.

Beth's mom stuck her head out the front door.

"She seems like a very nice girl," she said. "And it

makes me happy that you'll have a friend close to home. Now, young lady, back to the boxes!"

Beth climbed into the moving truck and picked up another box. She was starting not to mind so much that she had trouble remembering the past. Here she was in a nice new house, with her mom, and she'd already made a new friend.

Beth Picard was determined not to dwell on the past. From now on she would set her sights squarely on the future.

CHAPTER 2

ALMOST ONE YEAR LATER . . .

Beth raced down the hall, pausing every few seconds to look back over her shoulder.

She's still after me, Beth thought, picking up her pace.

It didn't make logical sense, but the faster Beth ran, the closer the girl in the mirror at the end of the hallway came toward her. And everywhere Beth turned, the mirror and the girl in it followed. Beth stopped short, but the girl in the mirror kept running, getting closer and closer. Spinning back around, Beth found herself staring into a blank wall, as if the hallway she had just come down had vanished.

Who is she . . . and why is she following me?

A door suddenly appeared on Beth's right. She yanked it open and sped through the doorway, slamming it behind her. Beth breathed a sigh of relief. But when she eyed the room she had just stepped into, she was faced with mirrors on every wall. Even the ceiling was totally covered in mirrors jutting out at every angle.

And in each mirror she saw the girl. She knew the girl. That much was certain. But how? From where? Who was she?

Suddenly, impossibly, one of the images of the girl popped out of a mirror in the ceiling and dropped to the floor in front of Beth. From this close, she recognized the girl. She looked exactly like Beth.

What is going on?

The girl said nothing but stared at Beth with a puzzled look on her face. Then she reached out suddenly, grabbed Beth's arm, and said, "You're coming with me!"

"Nooo!" Beth screamed.

When she stopped screaming, Beth realized that she was awake in her bed with her eyes wide open.

It was just another dream, she thought, as her heart pounded away in her chest. *Why do I keep having them?*

Rubbing her eyes and trying to shake the bad dream

from her mind, Beth climbed from her bed and walked to the bathroom. She had woken up only a few minutes before her alarm was about to go off. Soon it would be time to begin her daily homeschool lessons with her mom.

Bad dreams aside, Beth was happy in her new life. In the year that had passed since she and her mom had moved into their house, Beth had become comfortable with her routine: school lessons in the morning, hanging out with Chrissy in the afternoon, homework in the evenings, and then bed when her mom went to work and Joan, the overnight babysitter, arrived. Life was pretty good.

Especially because Beth and Chrissy had become great friends.

But the best part of the past year was the fact that Beth's memory problems seemed to have disappeared. She still couldn't conjure up memories from before the move, but she tried not to dwell on that, especially because everything that had happened to her during the past year, down to the tiniest detail, remained sharp in her mind.

She could remember the shapes of the snowflakes

during the first snowfall at her new house and building a snowman with Chrissy. She remembered the day they painted her bedroom a shiny purple and the day she decided she hated it and then repainted it lime green.

After breakfast that morning Beth and her mom settled down at the dining room table, books spread across its gleaming oak surface.

"Okay, let's go back to the chapter on Native American history," said Beth's mom, flipping open her book. "I think we left off with the evolution of the Cherokee Nation."

"Yup," said Beth. "Right here in chapter five, the 'Principal Chiefs of the Cherokee Nation.'"

"What can you tell me about the leaders of the Cherokee Nation East?" Beth's mom asked.

"Chief Black Fox was the first great leader of the Cherokee Nation East in the early 1800s," Beth reported. "He was one of the signers of the Holston Treaty and led the tribe for a decade."

"Excellent," her mom said.

Beth grinned proudly. Native American history was a topic that she really enjoyed.

"Let's move on to the Lakota," said her mother, but

Beth made no move to turn the page. "Beth, are you okay?"

"What?" Beth replied absentmindedly.

"Am I boring you?" her mom asked, sarcastically. "You're usually very interested in history."

"What? Oh, I'm sorry, Mom. I just had a thought that took me away for a minute. It's funny, but I know more about the history of people who lived hundreds of years ago than I do about my own history."

Beth's mom squirmed a bit in her seat. "But your memory has gotten much better," she said, unable to disguise the disappointment in her voice.

Beth felt bad, hearing her mother sound upset. She knew her mother wanted nothing more than for Beth to be happy, and she was. She just couldn't help but wonder about her past. She also wondered if her missing memories would haunt her for the rest of her life.

"You're right," she told her mom. "It has, as far as remembering the events since we've been here. But it still feels weird not to remember anything before that."

"I know, honey," Mom said, her tone now much more sympathetic. "That accident robbed you of a lot. But think of all you have now. A nice home. A good friend."

"Absolutely," Beth said, smiling. "Okay, no more feeling sorry for myself. Back to history."

When the morning's lessons were over, Beth and her mom took a ride into town for a shopping trip.

"I'm psyched about getting my new shoes," said Beth as she and her mom stepped into the local shoe store.

"Me too," said her mom. "I can't remember the last time I bought myself a pair of shoes."

Beth and her mom wandered through the aisles pulling out boxes of shoes.

"I love these!" Beth squealed, slipping on a pair of bright orange sneakers. "Chrissy has a pair just like them, and she said everyone at her school is wearing them."

Beth's mom rolled her eyes but then shrugged. "Okay," she said. "I'm glad *you* like them. Now it's my turn." She headed down the women's aisle.

"I need to run next door for some new sunglasses," Beth called out to her mother. "I'll be right back."

Beth's mom stopped what she was doing.

"Wait for me, please," she insisted, sounding uncharacteristically stern.

Beth sighed. "Whenever we go anywhere, you never let me out of your sight even for a minute. I'm not a baby, you know, Mom. Don't you trust me?"

"Of course I trust you, honey," Beth's mom replied. "It's just, you know, things can happen. What can I say? I'm a worrier. Please wait. I'll only be a couple of minutes."

"Oh, all right," Beth said. Now it was her turn to roll her eyes.

Chrissy's mom isn't overprotective like my mom is, she thought.

Beth slumped into a chair and stared out the window. She watched people walk by, thinking about how they could go where they wanted, when they wanted. She wished, for a moment, that she was someone else. Anyone else.

"Look at these, Beth," her mom said a few minutes later.

Beth turned back from the window. Her mom extended her feet, revealing a pair of white tennis shoes.

"What do you think?" she asked.

"You look like you're ready for a tennis match," Beth joked, smiling. "Either that, or you're going to work as a nurse."

"Well, I do work in a medical research lab, you know," her mom replied. "I'm on my feet a lot."

"I know, Mom," Beth said. "I'm just giving you a hard time. They're nice."

"Okay then," said her mom. "Let me pay for these and yours, and then we'll go next door together and get you some sunglasses."

When they returned home that afternoon, Beth's mom went to bed. She usually slept through the afternoon, before getting up to have dinner with Beth, then heading off to work.

Beth worked on her school assignments until three thirty. That's when Chrissy got home from school and they could hang out. Beth loved going to Chrissy's house, not just because they were such good friends, but because it was just about the only place Beth's mom ever let her go by herself.

"How was school today?" Beth asked as she walked into Chrissy's house.

Chrissy grimaced. "Some days I wonder how you can deal with being homeschooled and not being around lots of people. Then there are days like today, when Greg Hammer decided that it would be funny to smear his bubble gum all over my science book. Today I thought about how nice it must be to not have to deal with other people all the time."

"Bubble gum?" Beth asked. "Really? Did he get into trouble?"

"Of course not," Chrissy replied. "His older brother is the starting center on the high school basketball team, and Mr. Dunkins, my science teacher, is the assistant coach. So Greg got the usual fake-stern lecture about being mature, blah blah blah, and I got to scrape gum off my book. Really fair, right?"

"That sounds awful," Beth said. "The next time I start to feel sorry for myself about not going to a school every day, I'll try to remember that. Of course, remembering stuff is not exactly one of my strong suits."

"But that's not true anymore," Chrissy replied. "I know you don't remember a lot from before you moved next door—"

"I don't remember *anything*," Beth interrupted.

"Yeah, but you've actually got a better memory than I do since then," Chrissy pointed out. "I mean, you're the one who can name just about every river in the United States. You're the one who knows the name of each vice president."

"Well, I like history and geography, that's all," Beth said.

"Anyway, let's talk about something else. I have some news," said Chrissy, changing the subject.

"What? What?" Beth asked eagerly.

"My cousin Alice is sleeping over tomorrow night," Chrissy explained. "She's fourteen and lives in Glenside."

"That'll be fun for you," said Beth.

"And you! You're invited!" added Chrissy excitedly.

"Wow, thanks. That's very cool," said Beth. Then her mood instantly sank. "Now all I have to do is convince my mother to let me come."

"You'll be right next door," Chrissy said.

"I know that. *You* know that," said Beth. "But overnight? We've never done a sleepover before and that might be too much for her."

"It would be very cool if you could come," said Chrissy. "I think you'd really like Alice."

"I think it would be great," said Beth. She'd always wanted to go to a sleepover. She hadn't been to any in the past year, and she had no idea if she'd ever been to one before her accident.

"Let me ask my mom tomorrow morning," Beth

added. "She's usually in a really good mood when we start lessons for the day."

Chrissy clapped her hands and jumped up and down. "Great, then it's settled."

"No, settled is the last thing it is," said Beth. "I'll let you know."

"Okay. Now let's watch a movie," suggested Chrissy.

"Have anything in mind?" asked Beth.

"A scary one, of course!" Chrissy replied.

"Cool!" agreed Beth. She didn't really love scary movies, but she could see how excited Chrissy was to watch one.

"Have you seen *Creature from the Cellar*?"

Beth shook her head no.

"Oh, wow! Great! I could see that one a hundred times."

Chrissy and Beth sat on the floor in Chrissy's bedroom and leaned against the side of her bed. Chrissy flipped open her laptop and started streaming the movie on her computer.

In the movie two girls, not that different in age from Beth and Chrissy, were preparing a snack in the kitchen of an old house. They had set out four pieces of bread beside an open jar of jelly. Then one of the girls opened a cabinet. . . .

"Oh!" she cried. "No more peanut butter!"

"In the whole house?" exclaimed her friend. "That's horrific."

"No, silly," the first girl replied. "You know my mom. She buys like fifty jars at a time at the Giant Mart. I just have to go down to the cellar and grab another jar."

That's when the girls heard a sound—a low banging coming from down in the cellar.

"Is your brother home?" asked the girl's friend. "I thought we had the whole house to ourselves."

"We do."

"Then who is making that noise?"

Again they heard the banging, followed by a scraping sound, and then a low moan.

"This is crazy," said the girl. "I'm going down there to see what's going on! Plus, we still need peanut butter."

"Wait. You're going where?" asked her friend.

"To the cellar. It's my house. I know what's down there."

"But that's where the noise is coming from!"

"You don't have to come if you don't want, but I'm going to."

"Uh, I'll wait here and start putting the jelly on the bread."

"Okay, suit yourself."

The girl opened the old wooden door leading down to the cellar. She flipped on the light switch. Nothing happened. She flipped it up and down a few more times. Still nothing happened.

She snatched a flashlight from a small shelf at the top of the cellar stairs, turned it on, and let its narrow beam guide her way down the stairs.

Reaching the cellar floor, she swept the light from side to side, but saw nothing out of the ordinary.

The girl crossed the slate cellar floor, stepping around old boxes and unused furniture. She reached the storage pantry, grabbed the handle, and threw open the door

And that's when the scaly claw reached out from the dark and grabbed her wrist.

Upstairs in the kitchen, her friend was busy spreading jelly onto bread slices. After a few minutes she grew impatient and opened the cellar door.

"Rachael?" she called out.

Silence.

"Rachael!" she shouted a bit louder. Still no answer.

"Oh, great. Now I'm going to have to go down there!"

She took another flashlight and headed down the stairs.

"Why do they always go down into the cellar?" Chrissy asked Beth. "You know what's going to happen."

"No, I don't know," said Beth. "I haven't seen this before."

"Oh, come on," Chrissy teased.

"Shhh . . . there she goes," said Beth, and the girls turned their attention back to the computer screen.

The girl had reached the bottom of the stairs, which she had been illuminating with the flashlight. She raised her light to begin her journey across the cellar.

But she didn't get very far. Standing before her was a seven-foot-tall reptilian beast. Its claws sparkled in the light. One of Rachael's barrettes was stuck to its scaly skin. Drool dripped from its misshapen jaws.

"Yiiiiiiiii!"

Beth and Chrissy both let out high-pitched shrieks.

"Chrissy," her mom called from downstairs. "Are you watching scary movies again?"

Beth and Chrissy started laughing uncontrollably. Eventually they calmed down and went back to watching the movie. For the rest of the film they kept their screams as quiet as could be.

When the movie ended, Beth stood up. "Thanks, Chrissy, that was fun."

"Yeah," replied Chrissy. "That movie is the best and

also the worst. I hope your mom lets you come to the sleepover. We can watch more scary movies."

Beth nodded. "I hope so too."

"Text me tomorrow morning and tell me what she says," said Chrissy.

The next morning at breakfast Beth was quieter than usual. Finally she broached the subject she had been thinking about nonstop since she left Chrissy's house.

"Chrissy's cousin Alice is coming to visit today," Beth began, figuring she'd ease into the conversation slowly.

"That's nice," said her mom between bites of toast.

"And she'll be sleeping over," Beth explained.

"Uh-huh," her mom said.

She knows what's coming, Beth thought anxiously. *But here goes anyway.*

"And guess what?" Beth said excitedly.

Beth's mom looked up from her book.

"Chrissy invited me to join them for the sleepover," Beth said, flashing her biggest, brightest smile.

Her mom's shoulders sank. "Oh, honey, I don't know."

"Why not?" Beth asked, doing her best not to raise

her voice. She knew very well that escalating this conversation into an argument would get her nowhere. "It's just next door. You trust Chrissy's parents and Chrissy. You know what good friends we are."

Beth expected an argument, but her mom's expression turned to one of sadness more than anything else. She appeared lost in thought.

Beth ate another spoonful of her cereal as the silence continued for a few more uncomfortable seconds.

Her mom sighed. "Okay, you can go because it is only next door, and because Chrissy has been such a good friend," she said. "Joan will be excited to have a random night off."

Beth practically leaped from her seat. She gave her mom a big hug.

"Thanks, Mom!" she said.

"You'll be home by the time I get home from work tomorrow morning, right?" her mom asked.

"You bet!" Beth cried. "I'm going to go upstairs and pack."

"Aren't you forgetting something? The sleepover is twelve hours away. Right now it's time to hit the books."

Beth sat back down. "Oh yeah, right. Okay, let's get learning!"

The day's lessons dragged for Beth. All she could think about was the sleepover. When evening finally did roll around, Beth hummed happily as she packed. It took all her concentration not to burst into song from excitement.

"Do you have everything you need for tonight?" her mom questioned as she ran around the house, getting herself ready to go to work.

"Yes, Mom," Beth replied with as much patience as she could muster. She glanced down at her fully stocked backpack.

"Your pajamas?"

"Yes, Mom."

"Your toothbrush?"

"Yes, Mom."

"Sleeping bag?"

"That's what this big rolled-up thing next to my backpack is."

"Is your cell phone charged?"

"No."

Beth's mom gave her a look. Beth smiled. "Of course it is, and I'll bring my charger along just in case."

"You have my work number programmed in, right?"

"Since the minute I got the phone. Mom, I'm not going camping in Siberia. I'm just going next door."

"I know, honey. I know." She gave Beth a big hug. "Okay. Gotta go. Have fun. Lock the door on your way out. Call me if you need anything."

"Bye, Mom. Love you."

The front door closed behind her mother. Beth slumped down onto the stairs leading up to her bedroom and sighed. She couldn't understand why her mom was so overprotective. After all, Beth never got in trouble and she always told her mom everything. Not that there was much to tell. Her life was pretty boring.

"Oh well," she said aloud. "Time for my first sleepover!"

Beth snatched up her backpack and sleeping bag and headed over to Chrissy's. She stepped up to the front door and knocked. The door flew open, revealing Chrissy and another girl. A tall, skinny girl with long, straight brown hair.

"You must be Alice," said Beth. "Hi."

"Lizzie?" asked Alice, her eyes opening wide. "Is that you?"

CHAPTER 3

"Um, this is Beth, Alice," Chrissy corrected, looking at her cousin like she had two heads. "Who's Lizzie?"

Beth was startled. She was not used to being around any other kids besides Chrissy, and now she was meeting someone new who just asked if she was someone else.

"Lizzie . . . uh, I don't remember her last name," Alice replied. "She was in seventh grade with me at Glenside Middle School last year."

"Well, that's definitely not me," Beth said, walking into Chrissy's house. "I've always been homeschooled. I never went to Glenside."

"Really?" asked Alice as the three girls headed to the

stairs toward Chrissy's bedroom. "Hi, by the way."

"I swear," answered Beth. "And hi to you too."

Chrissy's mom and dad walked into the hallway from the living room.

"Hi, Mr. and Mrs. Walters," said Beth. "Thanks for having me over tonight."

"You are very welcome," said Mrs. Walters. "We're so pleased your mom allowed you to come."

Chrissy's parents really liked Beth and loved that she had become such a good friend to Chrissy. They also felt a little sorry for her, knowing about her accident and memory loss.

"Well, you girls have fun," said Mrs. Walters.

"Thanks, Mom," said Chrissy. Then the three girls ran upstairs.

When they got to Chrissy's bedroom, Beth unrolled her sleeping bag on the floor right next to Chrissy's and Alice's. Chrissy reached over to her MP3 dock and started her favorite playlist. Alice couldn't seem to take her eyes off Beth.

Beth wanted to like Alice, and she wanted to have fun at the sleepover, but two minutes into it she was beginning to regret begging her mother to let her come.

"I'm sorry to keep talking about this, but it's totally freaking me out," Alice said. "You must have a cousin, or a sister, or some relative who looks a lot like you."

"I don't think so," Beth said, feeling more uncomfortable by the second. Although she had, for the most part, made peace with her memory problems, moments like this, such as not knowing who might be part of her family, frustrated her to no end. "At least no one my mother ever told me about."

"This is so weird," Alice said. "Lizzie looked *just* like you."

Beth shrugged. As far as she knew, she had no family other than her mom. And it wasn't something she liked to think about. She was anxious for the subject to change. But Alice wasn't ready to let it go.

"I haven't thought about her in a long time, but Lizzie was kind of odd," Alice continued. "She wasn't in any of my classes at Glenside, but I remember her because she always sat alone at lunch. I felt bad for her so I tried to make friends with her one day. But she was super quiet, and I got the feeling she didn't want to be my friend. She just wanted to stay by herself."

"Great song choice, Chrissy," Beth said, referring

to what was coming through the dock's speakers, desperately trying to change the topic.

No such luck. Before Chrissy could say anything, Alice continued.

"Then one day, Lizzie just vanished," she said. "She never showed up at the lunch table, and I never saw her at school again. When I asked my teachers and my friends about her, they had no idea who I was talking about. It was like she never existed. So weird."

"Maybe you have a long-lost sister your mom never told you about," Chrissy suggested to Beth. "I mean with your memory problems and all, who knows?"

Beth started to wish that Chrissy hadn't invited her to the sleepover. If the whole night was going to be nothing but talking about how much some girl Alice once knew looked like her, and all of her past memory problems, Beth could live without it.

"So how long have you lived next door to Chrissy, Beth?" Alice asked.

Maybe she finally realized how uncomfortable all this Lizzie talk was making Beth feel, but whatever the reason, Beth was relieved that Alice had finally changed the subject.

"Almost a year," Beth replied.

"And we've been best friends since the day she moved in, right, Beth?" Chrissy asked.

"Right," said Beth.

"What's it like to be homeschooled?" Alice asked. "I think it could be kinda cool, but also a bit lonely."

"It's both," Beth said, warming up to Alice. "My mom's a great teacher. I love history and I learn a lot and it's fun. But I think it would also be fun to be with a bunch of other kids at school."

"Not everyone in school is as nice as Chrissy," Alice said. "Some days, I wish I was homeschooled just so I wouldn't have to deal with some of the other students at my school."

"Why does your mom want to homeschool you?" Chrissy asked.

Beth was a little surprised by the question until she realized that Chrissy had never actually asked her this before.

"My mom is super protective," Beth explained. "She almost never lets me out of her sight. I had to beg her just to be allowed to come here tonight. I think she'd have a nervous breakdown or something if I went off to school every day."

"How come she's so protective?" asked Alice.

Beth thought about this for a moment, but came up blank. She had no idea why her mom was the way she was. She had just always been that way, or at least since Beth's accident, and so her protectiveness seemed totally normal to Beth.

"Maybe it has something to do with my accident and memory loss," Beth figured. "Maybe she's just afraid something like that will happen again, and she's trying to protect me."

Beth looked away from the others for a moment. She felt different from other kids, and it made her sad. She was tired of talking about herself and her memories and all that stuff. It was time to get this sleepover underway.

"Anyway, enough about me," Beth said. "This is my first sleepover ever. So what do you do for fun at a sleepover?"

"Eat snacks," said Alice.

"Watch movies!" cried Chrissy.

"Great!" said Beth. "Let's get started."

The three girls headed to the kitchen. Chrissy opened the fridge and began pulling things out—bread, peanut butter, marshmallows, chocolate bars, cookies, a can of whipped cream. Next came the freezer and out came ice cream bars and ice pops.

Within a few minutes the three girls were hunkered down at the kitchen table building wild concoctions worthy of a team of mad scientists.

"Okay," said Chrissy. "I've got a peanut butter, ice cream, and chocolate bar sandwich topped with whipped cream."

"Sick, in a good way!" cried Alice. "Here's my marshmallow, chocolate chip cookie, and banana mash-up."

"I made a little building with ice pops as the sides, an ice cream sandwich as the roof, and animal crackers as the pets inside the house," said Beth.

"Ready, set, eat!" shouted Chrissy.

The three girls tore into their snacks as if they hadn't eaten in a week. When they finished, each of their faces was smeared with streaks of chocolate, drips of orange ice, and patches of whipped cream.

"Face stuffing complete!" announced Chrissy, sliding down in her chair.

"I don't think I'll eat again tonight," Beth said.

"I don't think I'll eat again this year!" added Alice.

"Movie time!" shouted Chrissy. "*Creature from the Cellar?*"

"Not again!" cried Beth.

"But Alice hasn't seen it yet!" Chrissy whined.

"It's pretty scary," said Beth.

"Cool, what are we waiting for?" asked Alice.

The three girls pried themselves away from the table and bounded back upstairs. They stretched out on their sleeping bags as Chrissy set up her laptop so they could all see the screen. Then she started streaming *Creature from the Cellar.*

When the movie ended, the girls chatted until they grew sleepy.

Just before she dropped off to sleep, Beth thought about how much fun she had had tonight, hanging out at a sleepover, just like a regular kid. Then she thought about that girl Lizzie and couldn't shake the idea that maybe she did have a sister that her mom had never told her about. She imagined what it might be like to grow up with a sister, possibly even a twin sister, and felt a rush of excitement mingled with disappointment.

And then she fell asleep.

"Lizzie! Hurry up. We'll be late for school."

Beth stood at the bottom of the stairs, her backpack slung over her shoulder. She glanced out the window and saw the school bus pulling up in front of her house.

"The bus is here! We're gonna be—"

"Hold your horses," shouted Lizzie.

She ran down the stairs, her feet barely touching each one, her auburn hair bouncing behind her, her freckles highlighted by the sun streaming through the window.

Lizzie looked exactly like Beth.

"Well, what are you waiting for?" Lizzie asked, rushing past Beth. She threw open the door and looked back over her shoulder. "You don't want to miss the bus do you, sis?"

Beth shook her head and laughed, then followed Lizzie out the door.

After scrambling up onto the school bus, Beth flopped down into a window seat, leaving the aisle seat open for Lizzie.

But Lizzie was not on the bus.

The bus driver started to close the door.

"Wait!" Beth shouted, dashing up to the front of the bus. "Wait for my sister!"

The bus driver looked at Beth as if she had lost her mind.

"Your sister?" the driver asked.

"Yeah, my sister, Lizzie," Beth stated flatly. "My *twin* sister? She looks exactly like me?"

"I've been picking you up at this house for a year," the driver explained, pulling the lever to close the door. "You are the only kid I've ever picked up at this house. Now take your seat or you're going to make everyone late."

Beth looked out the window, expecting to see Lizzie standing there getting ready to bang on the door.

No Lizzie.

She looked down the center aisle of the bus.

No Lizzie.

I have no sister, Beth realized.

That's when she woke up and saw that she was in her sleeping bag on the floor of Chrissy's bedroom. The whole Lizzie thing was just a dream.

I have no sister . . .

. . . or do I?

CHAPTER 4

When Beth opened her eyes the next morning, she glanced over at Chrissy and Alice, who were still sound asleep. The intense dream about Lizzie not only freaked her out and confused her, but it also sapped her energy and exhausted her. She soon fell back asleep.

By the time Beth woke up for good, Chrissy and Alice were already up and downstairs. Beth joined them in the kitchen, where at least six boxes of cold cereal were lined up on the table.

"Good morning, sleepyhead," said Chrissy. "Welcome to our Saturday morning breakfast feast."

"Yeah, pick your favorite three cereals, mix them together, then dig in," Alice added.

"Only three?" Beth asked, smiling. She grabbed a box of Honey-Crusted Crunchies and poured them into a bowl. The she stirred in Fruit-Flavored Roundies and Fun Flakes.

"Delicious!" she said, eating her first spoonful.

"That was a great movie last night!" said Alice through a mouthful of cereal.

"I'm going downstairs to get more peanut butter!" Beth said, mimicking the girl in the movie.

"Arrrrrgh!" Alice groaned, lifting her arms and curling her hands into claws, pretending to be the creature.

Chrissy giggled. "It was great having both of you sleep over," she said.

"It was so much fun," said Beth. Then her mind flashed back to her dream. She couldn't get Lizzie out of her mind.

"You okay?" Alice asked.

"Huh?" Beth replied, startled out of her thoughts.

"Your expression just changed, like you were worried about something," said Chrissy.

"Maybe you're worried about . . . the monster! Arrrrrgh!" Alice cried, doing her creature imitation again.

Beth smiled. "No, no, I'm fine," she lied.

After breakfast Beth rolled up her sleeping bag and packed up her backpack.

"Thanks again for inviting me, Chrissy," she said as she stuffed her pajamas into the pack. "I had a really great time."

"Yeah, we should do it again soon," said Chrissy.

"It was so great to meet you, Beth," added Alice. "I hope I see you again. And I hope I didn't upset you talking about that girl Lizzie. It was just a little weird for me to meet someone who looks just like someone else I used to know."

"Nice meeting you too, Alice, and don't worry about it," Beth said.

Alice and Beth exchanged e-mail addresses and phone numbers and talked about hanging out again soon.

"See ya later," said Chrissy, as Beth headed out the front door.

On the short walk home Beth thought about the fact that Chrissy and Alice would be going to school on Monday. She felt a pang of sadness that she would not be going too. She pictured, not for the first time, what it might be like to go to school with other kids.

Then she shook her head, as if answering her own thoughts.

You've got it pretty good here, she thought as she headed through her front door. *You've got a mom who loves you and is a great teacher. You've got a best friend who lives right next door. And your memory seems to be working pretty well these days. So quit feeling sorry for yourself. There are plenty of girls who are way worse off than you are.*

Beth set her laptop and schoolbooks on the dining room table. Her mom would be home from work in about an hour. She had gotten all caught up on her schoolwork before going over to Chrissy's house yesterday, so she was all ready for today's lessons. Even though it was Saturday, there were still lessons to be learned—one of the downsides of being homeschooled.

But Beth could not get Lizzie out of her mind. The dream she had had last night still haunted her. What if she did have a sister and just didn't remember? Why would her mom keep something like that from her? She had to know.

Beth began searching online for any information or pictures of girls named Lizzie who went to Glenside Middle School last year. She scanned as many search results as she could before her eyes went blurry but found no matches.

She was almost ready to give up, to shove this mystery to the dark corners of her mind to join all the other unanswered questions she had about her life, when a noise sounded on her laptop, indicating that she had just received a new e-mail.

The e-mail was from Alice.

The subject read: *Picture of Lizzie . . . kinda*

Beth anxiously opened the e-mail and downloaded the picture. When she clicked it open, a photo filled her screen. It showed a school cafeteria crowded with middle school students.

At the center of the photo Alice and a group of her friends were clowning around for the camera. Beth assumed that this must be the cafeteria at Glenside Middle School. She stared at the shot but couldn't figure out why Alice would have sent it to her. And why did the e-mail subject refer to Lizzie?

That's when Beth read the short message in the body of the e-mail:

Zoom in, top right.

Beth quickly opened her photo-editing program and

imported the shot. She drew a frame around the top right section and then clicked the zoom tool. The image within the frame grew large. She clicked zoom again. The image grew even bigger.

A final click revealed that among the frenzied chaos that was the school cafeteria, one girl, way in the background, sat alone at a table. Beth created another frame around the girl's face and zoomed in on that.

She was instantly overcome by a sickly feeling. Staring at the enlarged face in disbelief, Beth realized that she was looking at a picture of herself. Or rather, someone who looked exactly like her—same auburn hair, same freckles, and same brown eyes.

Lizzie is real. And Alice is right—she does look exactly like me!

At that moment Beth's mom walked through the front door, having arrived home from work. Beth quickly closed her laptop.

"Hi, honey, how was the sleepover?" Mom asked, joining Beth at the dining room table. "I didn't get a panicked phone call so I assume everything went well."

"Hi, Mom." Beth greeted her. "I had a great time.

We made some delicious snacks and watched movies and laughed a lot. Didn't get much sleep though. I don't get why they call them 'sleepovers.' Not much sleeping going on."

"And what about Chrissy's cousin, Alice? Was she nice?"

"I liked her a lot," Beth replied. "We're going to try to stay in touch."

"Great," said Mom. "Okay, then. Enough chitchat. Time to hit the books."

As Beth opened her history textbook and pulled up the paper she had written on her laptop, she turned and looked right at her mom.

"Do I have a sister?" Beth blurted out suddenly. She surprised herself by the directness of the question.

"What do you mean?" her mom asked in a shocked tone of voice.

"I mean, do I have a sister you never told me about?" Beth repeated.

"What brought this on?" her mom asked anxiously.

Before she answered, Beth thought about what she should say next. The question seemed to have made her mother uncomfortable. And that made Beth think that her mother was hiding something. After all, she hadn't answered with a simple yes or no.

"When Chrissy's cousin, Alice, first saw me, she thought I was someone else," Beth explained.

"What do you mean, 'someone else'?" replied her mom.

Beth explained. "Alice goes to school at Glenside Middle School. She said there was this girl in her class last year named Lizzie and she looked exactly like me. Like she was my sister or even my twin."

Her mom shook her head. "Come on, honey, lots of people look like other people. It's so common, there's even a word for someone who looks just like you, but isn't your twin. Doppelgänger."

Beth eyed her mother warily. Nothing her mother had said had convinced Beth that she was telling her the truth. Beth turned the laptop screen toward her mom and brought up the zoomed-in photo of Lizzie in the cafeteria.

Beth's mom stared at the photo for a second, her face betraying no emotion.

"That picture's kind of fuzzy, don't you think?" Mom asked. "Sure that girl has auburn hair and freckles, but so do lots of girls."

"Mom, she's a dead ringer for me," Beth insisted.

"That's a little bit of an exaggeration, I think," Mom said. "Now let's get to something important—your schoolwork."

Beth turned to her schoolwork but felt highly unsatisfied with her mom's explanation of why this Lizzie person looked so much like her. It was clear that she was not going to get any help from her mom in figuring out this mystery.

Beth Picard realized that she would have to take matters into her own hands.

CHAPTER 5

In the days and weeks that followed Beth continued to obsess about Lizzie. And the more Beth pondered the mystery girl, the more she began to question just how very little her mom had told her about her life before moving into this house. Beth had been told that she'd had an accident, and that her memories of all that happened up to the accident, as well as of the accident itself, were gone, most likely forever.

But why had her mom not done her best to feed those memories to her? Why hadn't her mom talked to her every day about her early life so that Beth would have a larger sense of who she was, where she came from, and how she grew to be the person she was now? Certainly her mom had been there. *She* must have memories of Beth's first twelve years, yet she chose not to share them.

For some reason these thoughts had never actually occurred to Beth before this whole Lizzie thing started. And now she had come to the conclusion that her mom was intentionally keeping things from her.

Sure, her mom had said, *Why dwell on the past? You're young. You've got a long, bright future ahead of you. Focus on that. Let go of those lost memories. They can't do you any good, even if I recited them to you over and over. They still wouldn't actually be yours.*

That argument had always sounded logical to Beth so she had gone with it and kept her sights focused on the future and moving forward.

But these days that argument just sounded like a lie, an excuse, a justification for hiding something. It was a way to keep Beth from knowing who she really was. She had always wondered about her past but had no idea how to start to find out any details.

Now she had a starting place: Lizzie. And she couldn't pass up a chance to finally learn the truth about who she was.

Each day, once her mom was asleep or had gone to work, Beth searched her house or trolled the far corners of the Internet hoping to find the link she had been missing, the link that would bring her the facts behind Lizzie . . . and her own life.

She hit a blank every time.

If Lizzie does exist, she's covered that fact pretty well, thought Beth. *Maybe she's a spy! Maybe she's purged her identity from the Internet.*

Beth leaned back and took a deep breath. She began to form an idea.

She had only one lead. She would have to follow that lead. And that lead was the student records at Glenside Middle School. Surely they had to have some record of a student who attended their school just the previous year. But how in the world would she ever be able to get inside to poke around? Somehow she had to figure that out.

One random weekday afternoon Beth was hanging out at Chrissy's house. They were checking out videos on the new tablet Chrissy had received from her parents.

Beth had kept her desire to go to Glenside to herself, but she couldn't hold it in any longer. She felt as if she had to share it with her best friend, or else she would absolutely explode.

"So, remember when Alice and I slept over?" Beth asked when a video they were watching had ended, realizing how dumb the question sounded as soon as it left her mouth.

"Yep. It was only a couple of weeks ago," Chrissy said.

"Yeah, I know," said Beth. "What I meant was, well, I haven't been able to stop thinking about Lizzie."

"Who?" asked Chrissy.

"The girl that Alice thought I looked like when she first saw me," Beth reminded her.

"Oh, that. Sure, I remember, but you seemed to be in a big hurry to change the subject so I put it out of my mind, and I haven't thought about it since."

"Well, I have," said Beth. "Thought about it, that is. All the time."

"Why? What's the big deal about someone looking like you?" asked Chrissy.

"This," said Beth, swinging the screen of her laptop around to show Chrissy the blown up version of the photo Alice had sent her.

"Wow!" Chrissy gasped. "She really is your twin."

"Right?" replied Beth. "Maybe literally, in fact. Although that would be really weird to have a twin named Lizzie. Beth and Lizzie are both the same name really. Nicknames for Elizabeth."

"Hmm, what did your mom say about all this?" asked Chrissy.

"That's the thing. She shrugged it off like there's only a tiny resemblance. But you see it. There's no doubt."

Chrissy nodded her head.

"So since I can't remember anything about growing up," Beth continued, "it's possible that Lizzie is related to me, or at least could tell me about the past . . . my past."

Chrissy nodded. "But why would your mom keep that from you?"

"I have no idea," answered Beth honestly. "She seems to get really bent out of shape whenever I bring it up. When I bring up anything about my past, she gets all tense and quiet."

"Have you looked Lizzie up online?" asked Chrissy.

"Every single day," said Beth. "In every way there is to search. Nothing. Can't find a single thing about a girl named Lizzie who was in seventh grade at Glenside last year."

Chrissy looked at Beth sympathetically. "So what are you gonna do?"

Beth sighed. "The only thing I can do—follow the one lead that Alice gave me."

"What's that?" asked Chrissy.

"I've got to go to the place Alice met her, Glenside Middle School," said Beth. "I've got to get inside, and I've got to search through their student records. Maybe I can get a last name for Lizzie, or where she's going to eighth grade this year. Maybe she was put up for adoption and has a new family. Maybe, if I'm really lucky, I can even find her address."

Chrissy looked shocked at hearing Beth's plan. "And maybe you can get in trouble for snooping around in private student records at a school you don't even go to!"

Beth knew Chrissy had a point, but there was something even more important that Beth had to try to find out. "Chrissy, I have to know if I have a sister. Maybe she can help me get back my memories, or at least tell me about them."

"I thought you had moved past all that. I thought you were all about the future now, not the past," said Chrissy.

Beth folded her arms. "I am. At least I thought I was."

Even Beth was surprised at the sense of urgency she felt. Before meeting Alice, hearing about Lizzie, and, especially, seeing the photo, Beth believed that she had made peace with her mysterious past. But now finding out the truth dominated her thoughts.

"So how are you going to do it?" Chrissy asked Beth. "And when? Your mom watches you like a hawk."

"Next Saturday she has an all-day meeting at work," Beth explained. "She's never had to work on a weekend before since she started this new job, but the whole staff has to be at this meeting. She'll be leaving for work on Friday evening and won't be home until Saturday night. My babysitter, Joan, will be staying over Friday night as usual, but she can't watch me on Saturday, so I'll be home alone after Joan leaves and before my mom gets back. Saturday's the day I've got to do it."

"Okay, so you have the *when*," said Chrissy. "What about the *how*? Glenside is all the way across town, and you don't even know how to ride a bike."

"I'm working on that," said Beth.

"What have you got so far?"

Beth stared at the wall and said nothing.

"I'll take that as an 'I've got nothing,'" said Chrissy.

"I've got nothing," Beth repeated. "But I've got a week to come up with a plan."

"I left food for you in the fridge," said Beth's mom the following Friday evening as she got ready to head off to work. Joan, Beth's babysitter, was running a little late and wouldn't arrive until after Beth's mom had to leave.

"Thanks, Mom," said Beth.

"And here's a list of phone numbers," Mom continued. "Doctors, the local police station, the fire department, poison control— "

"Are you expecting a disaster or something?" Beth asked. "I'll only be by myself for an afternoon."

"Here's some cash in case you need it," Mom continued, ignoring Beth's quip as she shoved papers into her briefcase and handed Beth some money. "Keep your cell phone on. Don't leave the house, and—"

"Mom!" yelled Beth.

Beth's mom looked up from rummaging through her purse. "What?"

"Go to work," said Beth, smiling. "Go to your meeting tomorrow. I'll be fine."

Mom sighed deeply. She smiled and gave Beth a big hug.

"I know you'll be fine, honey," she said, heading for the front door. "I'll see you tomorrow night."

Beth blew her a kiss. Then, just before she disappeared out the door, her mom leaned back in and said, "Did I remember to tell you that I left food for you in the fridge?"

Beth tossed and turned in bed that night. She was still up when she heard Joan go to bed in the guest room that doubled as Joan's room on the nights she babysat. Beth was worrying about just how she'd get into the student records room at Glenside Middle School the next day. She knew that tomorrow would be her one and only shot at trying to discover a clue to break open the mystery of just who she was.

The school would probably be empty since it would be Saturday, and that might mean it could also be locked. Slipping into a school she didn't belong to on a day when no students were there was one thing. Breaking and entering was a whole other thing, and something she wanted no part of.

Maybe someone will be there, Beth thought. *Maybe someone will be there cleaning the school, or the teachers have a meeting or something. Maybe a door will be unlocked.*

Finally, still without a clear plan in mind, she dozed off to sleep.

"Beth!"

A faint voice pierced Beth's sleep.

"Beth!" someone called again, louder this time.

Beth stirred in her bed. *Mom,* she thought. *What did she forget to tell me? That I'm supposed to breathe and eat and—*

"BETH!" someone screamed from downstairs.

Beth bolted upright in her bed. That wasn't her mom's voice or Joan's. She threw on a sweatshirt and walked quickly to the top of the stairs.

"Hello!" she called down.

No reply.

"Who's there?" she shouted.

Still silence.

"I guess the voice was in a dream," she mumbled, then she turned to head back to bed.

"Beth!" She heard the voice again.

"All right," she said, slowly turning back. "I'm definitely not asleep now."

Beth climbed down the stairs, her mind racing. *Who could be in the house? And why am I going downstairs alone?*

Despite not having answers to these questions, she continued. Reaching the bottom of the stairs, Beth flipped on the hall light.

She saw no one.

"Beth," someone said, now in a mere whisper.

"Who's there?" Beth called out. "Who's in my house?"

No reply.

Beth moved slowly down the hall in the direction of the voice.

"Where are you?" she called out. "Who are you?"

"Beth," came a faint cry from the living room.

Beth turned the corner at the far end of the hall and stepped into the living room. What she saw there startled and confused her.

Every wall in the room was covered with a full-length mirror. Mirrors also hung suspended from the ceiling and lined the floors.

This is all wrong, Beth thought. *There are no mirrors in my living room.*

What disturbed Beth more than the sudden appearance of all these mirrors was the image contained in each one.

Staring out from each silvered surface was Beth herself.

Or was it Lizzie?

Even stranger was the fact that each girl Beth saw in each mirror was dressed differently and doing something different. One combed her hair. One read a book. One kicked a soccer ball. None of them were actually a reflection of Beth. They were more like windows than mirrors—Beth was looking into windows showing other people, other lives.

And then the strangest thing yet happened. As Beth stared at each image, she suddenly found herself remembering doing the things she saw in the mirrors. She had a vivid flash of memory in which she scored the winning goal in a soccer game. A rush of pride and exhilaration flooded through her as if the event had just happened.

I remember that! But how? I have no memories other than the past year, and I've never played soccer. Yet I can recall every tiny detail of that goal!

Turning her head to glance into another mirror,

Beth spotted one of the girls blowing out candles at a birthday party. She stood at a table crowded with kids and leaned over to reach the cake.

My birthday party! she thought. *I remember that cake. I remember that purple dress I was wearing. I loved that dress. I remember feeling so loved, so happy that everyone was there for me.*

Beth watched herself blow out the candles. Curls of black smoke rose from the charred wicks. She got an instant sense memory and could smell the smoke right then, right there in her living room, in the middle of the night.

How can this be?

Looking down into a mirror on the floor, Beth stared wide-eyed as she saw herself step out of the main entrance to a hospital. She grasped someone's hand, but she couldn't see enough of the person to clearly make out whose it was.

I remember leaving the hospital, but I don't remember being sick. Is that my mom holding my hand. Could this be right after my accident?

Beth shook her head and rubbed her eyes.

How can I remember these things? I have no memories before this year, yet I am recalling all these things perfectly. I actually remember experiencing them, and not just vague memories, but feelings, smells, and sounds. This is impossible!

As if reacting to her thoughts, the images in the mirrors decided to take impossible to the next level. One by one the girls in the mirrors stepped out of the glass, like two-dimensional paper dolls come to life.

Beth backed away. Every nerve in her body told her to run, yet something kept her from bolting. A strange curiosity mingled with her fear, coupled with the overwhelming desire for answers, as if somehow these walking mirror people might be the key to unlocking her hidden past.

The girls stepped clumsily toward Beth. Several popped up from the mirrors on the floor, breaking free from the surface of their glass prisons, like swimmers stepping from silver ponds.

"Who are you?" Beth screamed. "What is happening?"

Moving as if they were connected as one being, the mirror girls each raised a hand and pointed at Beth.

"Me?" she asked. "You are all me?"

The girls drew their arms back toward their bodies, and each girl embraced herself in a hug. Then suddenly every mirror girl in the room toppled over, smashing to the floor, exploding in a shower of glass slivers.

Beth stared down in horror at the pile of broken glass in the center of her living room.

CHAPTER 6

Beth opened her eyes. She was in her bed, in her room.

Another strange dream.

She propped herself up on one elbow and turned toward her dresser. Catching a glimpse of herself in the mirror, she gasped. The image in the mirror did exactly the same thing.

That's a real mirror in the real world, she thought, trying to calm down, *not a crazy mirror from the crazy world in your dreams.*

Dreams. Now that her dream had ended, Beth could not summon a single memory from her past, not even those that were so vivid in the dreams. She recalled the weirdness with the mirrors and had a vague sensation of having remembered specifics from her life, but now they were gone. As if they only existed in her dreams.

She glanced at her alarm clock.

Saturday morning, 7:33 a.m. She might as well get up. She only had one shot to get into the Glenside Middle School records, and she still didn't really have a plan. All she knew was that she had to get into that school.

Beth showered, got dressed, and made herself some breakfast. At eight thirty Joan left. Before she did, she made Beth repeat what she'd promised to her mom as well: She wouldn't go anywhere. She wouldn't even open the door. Not for any reason.

As Beth munched on a piece of toast, she considered her options.

I'm twelve years old, just like all the other seventh graders who attend the school. I could be going there on a Saturday because I left an important book there, or because I have a special meeting with a teacher, or because a club that I was a member of had a weekend meeting. I should be able to walk into Glenside just like I belong there. But then again, nobody will know me.

Beth sighed. What other choice did she have? She had to go for it.

She loaded her camera, phone, laptop, directions on

how to walk to Glenside from her house, and a print-out of the photo of Lizzie into her backpack. Then she slipped out the front door and headed down her block. She was grateful that it was a warm, sunny day. It was at least a two-hour walk to Glenside, and Beth was happy she wouldn't have to do it in the rain or cold.

It didn't take her long to realize that she really had never been out in the world on her own before. Any trips she made to town were with her mom or in a car with her mom driving, so she never really had to pay attention to where she was going.

The farther from home Beth got the more lost she became. Soon nothing looked familiar—no streets, no houses, no stores. She believed that she was heading in the direction of Glenside Middle School, but she grew anxious.

What if I get lost and I'm not home before Mom? Beth worried. *Don't be ridiculous. Mom won't be home until tonight.*

She tried to calm herself down, but she was not doing a very good job.

Beth kept walking. At each intersection she debated with herself which way to turn. Confused, she considered turning around, going home, and just giving up her quest.

But something drove her to keep moving forward.

Might as well keep going, she thought.

She continued. And continued to have no idea where she was.

After about a half hour, the feeling started—the feeling that someone was following her.

Beth stopped and glanced over her shoulder but saw no one. She turned back and continued.

Beth took a few steps forward and turned back again. Still no one there.

Walking faster now, she heard a voice call out.

"Bess! Hey, Bess!" the voice shouted from behind her.

Beth turned around and saw a girl a few years older than she. The girl smiled and waved at her.

"Bess, how are you?" the girl asked.

Beth felt legitimately frightened now. She realized just how foreign it felt to be away from home. And it didn't help that she was lost. And now a total stranger thought she was someone else, for the second time this month!

She turned back and walked away even more quickly than before, not sure where she was going, but certain that she just wanted to be away from this girl.

"Snob!" the girl yelled after her. "You're too good for me now? I haven't seen you in years and you can't even say hello?"

Beth kept walking. She felt bad that the girl thought she was being snobby, but she had bigger things on her mind, and the last thing she needed was another mystery to solve related to her past.

At least I know that I'm not going crazy, she thought. *Someone really was following me.*

But even after Beth had lost the girl who called her Bess, she still felt like she was being followed. She caught the sound of footsteps scraping on pavement, but when she spun around to confront whoever might be there, she saw no one.

Beth picked up her pace, hoping both to get to the school sooner and to put some distance between her and whoever might be after her.

The feeling of being watched gripped her like a pair of hands. Again she spun around. This time she caught a glimpse of something or someone disappearing behind a nearby row of bushes.

"Who's there?" she called out, surprising herself with her boldness. "Why are you following me?"

But she only received silence in response.

On Beth walked, feeling more uneasy with every step.

What am I doing? she chastised herself. *I don't know where I'm going. I don't know what I'm going to do when I get there . . . if I get there. And someone is still following me. I just know it.*

BRRIIIIIIIIINGG!!

Beth's phone rang suddenly, startling her. She let out a short shriek, then fished around in her backpack and pulled out her phone. The caller ID read MOM.

Beth answered the call. She was grateful that it was quiet on this street so that her mom wouldn't suspect she wasn't at home.

"Hi, Mom. How's it going there?" she said as cheerily as she could.

"Great. Work is done and I'm about to start my meeting," said Mom. "How are things at home?"

"Fine. I had my breakfast, and I'm just starting to continue reading about the history of the Cherokee Nation."

At that moment a big truck rumbled down the street right past Beth.

"What's that noise?" Mom asked.

"Oh, a truck just went by," Beth replied. "I have the window open."

"Well, don't leave the window open all day," her mom warned. "I heard that it might rain later."

"Okay, Mom," said Beth, trying to rush off the phone. "Don't worry about me. Go have a nice meeting!"

"Okay, I'll check in with you later. Don't forget to eat lunch."

"Mom, when have I ever forgotten to eat lunch?" Beth replied. "Good-bye!"

Beth's mom said good-bye.

Beth hung up and breathed a sigh of relief.

She was about to slip her phone back into her pack when she paused and stared at the screen for a moment, remembering that her phone had GPS built right into it. She'd never used it before, but certainly she could figure it out.

She quickly scanned through all the apps on her phone and found the GPS program. She launched it and typed in *Glenside Middle School*. A few seconds later street-by-street directions appeared on her screen. Everything seemed so much clearer than the directions she had copied earlier that morning.

"I'm actually only a few blocks away, after all," she said, sounding surprised that her sense of direction had served her fairly well. With the GPS to guide her, Beth walked briskly now, moving with confidence. She would at least make it to Glenside. What happened after that was anyone's guess. Following the turns shown on her GPS, she moved closer to her destination.

And yet, she still could not shake the feeling that she was being followed.

Am I just paranoid because I'm nervous about slipping into a school where I don't belong? Beth wondered.

A few minutes later Beth made a right turn and Glenside Middle School appeared, just a few blocks ahead. Glenside was one of the older schools in the area. Its sturdy-looking redbrick walls gave it a classic feel, like a school Beth's mom might have attended once upon a time.

Trying to appear as casual as possible, Beth strode toward the school. The closer she got the harder her heart pounded. She could feel herself start to sweat.

She pictured what this place must look like on a typical school day with buses pulling up and kids pouring out onto the grounds. She wondered if it might have been easier to sneak into the building on a day when hundreds of kids were going in.

Not that she had any choice. This was a rare occasion when her mom was gone all day. She had to get this done today. She might never get another chance.

As she approached the school parking lot, she noticed that about a dozen cars were parked there. *All those cars must mean that there are some people at the school today, otherwise the lot would be empty. This is promising.*

Her spirits lifted a bit. If people were in the school working today, then at least one of the doors would be open. Step one had always been getting inside the school. Beth would figure out what came next once she was inside.

She was almost there. The front door grew larger with each step.

I'm gonna make it, Beth thought, a surge of excitement pulsing through her veins.

And that is when she spotted a uniformed security guard running from the far side of the school toward the front door.

Oh no. I'm so busted. He's coming for me! He knows. Somehow he knows!

Beth kept on walking.

What if he's after someone else? What if this has nothing to do with me?

She was almost at the front door.

But what if he is after me?

Panic took over. Beth turned and ran. She didn't turn back to see if the guard was after her or not. Her only thought was to get as far away from the school as she could.

She dashed down the few blocks leading away from school, feeling scared, sad, and confused. She made the left turn to start the journey home, crashed right into someone, and tumbled to the ground.

CHAPTER 7

"Are you okay?" asked a tall girl with short black hair and smooth, freckle-less skin. The girl leaned over Beth, looking down at her. Beth was sprawled on her back on the sidewalk.

"I think so," Beth answered. "I'm more stunned than hurt, actually. I didn't expect anyone to be there when I ran around that corner."

"Same here," said the girl, who reached down and offered Beth her hand.

Beth took the girl's hand.

"Are *you* okay?" Beth asked as the girl helped her up to her feet.

"Yeah, fine," the girl replied. "I'm Elizabeth, by the way."

"Beth," she said, brushing herself off. "Hey, we have the same name, kinda. Nice to meet you. Other than crashing into you, I mean."

"You seem to be in a big hurry," observed Elizabeth. "Or like you were running away from somebody."

Beth suddenly remembered the security guard who had been chasing her, or so she had thought. She looked back over her shoulder in a panic. "It's a long story. Really what I need is to get into the school," she explained.

"I go to school here, but I don't recognize you," said Elizabeth.

"That's 'cause I'm actually homeschooled," Beth explained. "I'm just trying to find someone who used to go to Glenside. And I believe that the only way to track her down is to search the school's records."

"Track her down, huh?" said Elizabeth. "That sounds pretty serious."

Beth admitted the reason behind her search. "I think she could be my twin sister, even though I've never met her."

"Kind of a 'separated at birth' type of thing?" asked Elizabeth.

"Something like that," replied Beth. "So what are you doing here on a Saturday?"

"I live nearby," Elizabeth explained. "I was just taking a walk."

"Well, I should be going," said Beth, looking back toward the building. "I still have to figure out a way to get in." Beth didn't want to be rude to Elizabeth, but she had to complete her mission.

"Oh, I can help you with that," said Elizabeth. "There are always a few teachers, administrators, and janitors at school on Saturdays. If you had tried the front door, you would have found it locked. The school staff uses a side door. That one should be open."

"You'll really help me?" Beth asked, feeling another surge of hope. "Even though we just met?"

"Hey, if I had a long-lost sister, you bet I'd do anything I could to find her. Come on."

Elizabeth turned the corner and started walking toward the school.

Beth followed, though she wasn't sure that this was going to work.

"What about the security guard?" Beth asked. "I think he might have been chasing me."

"I don't see him," said Elizabeth, pointing ahead to the school.

The security guard was nowhere in sight. Maybe he had been following someone else.

Unless, of course, he was hiding, waiting for Beth.

Beth continued walking with Elizabeth toward the school. *This may be my best chance,* Beth thought, looking around, searching for the guard or some other obstacle that might once again keep her from learning the truth.

"So, let me ask you, Elizabeth," Beth said as the two girls walked side by side. "You go to Glenside. Did you know a girl who went to school here last year and looks like me? I mean, looks exactly like me? Her name was Lizzie. I don't know her last name."

"No. Like I said, I don't recognize you at all."

As the girls approached the school, Beth felt her heart beat faster.

Stay calm. Stay calm, she repeated to herself.

"This way," said Elizabeth. "Around the side."

Beth followed Elizabeth through the parking lot and around to the far side of the building. Behind a grove of tall trees Beth spotted a small red door.

"That's it," said Elizabeth. "Let's try it."

"What if someone's right there?" Beth asked, her heart pounding once again.

"Then this is going to be a very short adventure!" Elizabeth said, chuckling.

Elizabeth grabbed the doorknob and turned it.

Beth heard the telltale click of an unlocked door. Elizabeth opened the door slowly and stepped inside. Beth took a deep breath, then followed.

Walking into a narrow hallway, Beth was struck by the fact that she had never actually been inside a school before, or at least she had no memory of having been in one. She looked around at the greenish-yellow cinder-block walls, peeling paint on all the doorframes, and grease-stained windows.

This is kinda creepy! she thought. *I don't know if I would like coming here every day. I never really appreciated how hard my mom works to teach me, how great a situation I have, and how much I really learn.*

As she and Elizabeth walked deeper into the school, Beth found herself suddenly racked with guilt.

If Mom ever found out where I am, what I am doing . . .

"Beth?"

Elizabeth's voice pulled Beth out of her maze of thoughts.

"You okay?"

"Yeah, sorry," replied Beth. "This is just all so new to me."

"So did you want to go to the records room?" asked Elizabeth. "I can tell you where it is."

"Thanks. That would be great," replied Beth.

BRIIIIIIIINNNGGGGGG!!!

The bell signaling that all students had to be in their classrooms blared through the empty halls, startling Beth.

"Why is that bell ringing on a Saturday?" Beth wondered.

"I guess it's programmed to go off at the same time each day, whether or not students are in the building," Elizabeth explained.

"So where are the records kept?" Beth asked, trying to focus again on the task.

"Take your next right and the next two lefts and you'll see the records room," Elizabeth said quickly. "I've got to get home. My mom is expecting me. Good luck, Beth. I hope you find your sister!"

Elizabeth turned and hurried back down the hallway, disappearing around a corner and leaving Beth alone in the empty hall.

"A right and two lefts," Beth repeated to herself.

Thank you, Elizabeth, she thought. *Whoever you are.*

Beth walked quickly, glancing back to make sure no one saw her.

This looking over my shoulder is getting to be a habit, she thought. *And not one I like.*

Beth took the first right, then a left. She felt anxious, as if the greenish-yellow walls were closing in as she hustled along.

One more left, and then—

"Hey! What are you doing here?" shouted someone behind her. "There are no student activities today!"

Beth spun around and saw a balding man in a tie and sports jacket walking briskly toward her.

Beth bolted around the corner and dashed down the hallway. She could hear the man's footsteps closing in on her.

At the end of the hall Beth spotted several storage cabinets. On the floor next to the cabinets sat opened boxes of ceiling tiles. Above the boxes several ceiling tiles were missing, creating an opening in the ceiling.

Reaching the cabinets, Beth flung open the door and began climbing up the metal shelves, using them as if they were rungs on a ladder. Scrambling onto the top of the cabinet, Beth reached up and grabbed the opening in the ceiling on either side.

Launching herself straight up, she pressed down on her palms, lifting her body up through the opening. She slipped above the ceiling tile and rolled onto her side.

Glancing back down, Beth saw the man who had been chasing her pass by underneath. The sound of his footsteps faded until they trailed away to silence.

Beth caught her breath and looked around at the space into which she had crawled. The thick layer of dust that covered the tops of the tiles now also covered her shirt and jeans. Electrical conduit snaked through the crawl space in every direction, forming a nest of metal strands.

And then something moved.

A small black circle scurried along right next to Beth's leg. A spider.

The spider stopped, as if to examine this invader of its domain. It raised its front two legs, rubbing them together, pondering its next move.

The spider crawled onto her jeans—

Don't move, don't move . . .

—and then crawled back off.

Mustering her courage while fighting the urge to

throw up from nerves, Beth lowered her head down through the opening. The hall was empty.

Shifting her position and getting covered with even more dust in the process, Beth swung her feet out of the hole. Grasping the edges of the ceiling opening, she supported her weight and lowered herself down to the top of the cabinet. She climbed down shelf by shelf, until she was back on the floor.

Dusting her clothes off as best as she could, she hurried toward the final leg of her journey. Turning left, she saw a row of offices. Each office had a sign that jutted out from the wall, making it easy to read.

The signs read PRINCIPAL, ASSIST. PRINCIPAL, ADMIN. ASSIST., MAINTENANCE.

And the last sign, at the far end of the hall, read STUDENT RECORDS.

That's it! Now all I have to do is make it past all these other offices.

Glenside Middle School had been built a long time ago, and that explained the dingy walls and windows, the old-fashioned ceiling tiles, and the overall gloomy atmosphere.

But it also explained why the door to each of these

offices was divided in half, like the door to a horse stall in a barn. The bottom half was closed and had a small shelf that formed its top board. The top half of each door was open so that a person could speak with the school administrators inside, and even pass along papers, without actually walking into the office.

Beth dropped to her knees, making sure she stayed below the opening above the bottom door, and crawled as quickly as she could down the hall, hugging the wall, remaining invisible to the people in the offices.

One by one she passed offices containing the most powerful people in the school—the school she didn't even go to. Just as she reached the door to the administrative assistant's office, she heard the knob on the bottom section of the door start to turn.

Beth froze mid-crawl.

"I'll bring these forms over to Ms. Dawkins," said a voice right above Beth.

The door started to open. She'd be discovered, and worse, her mom would find out what she had done. She held her breath.

"Later, Ralph," called another voice from inside the office. "She doesn't need them until next week, and we've got to finish compiling these test results."

"Okay," said Ralph.

The door closed.

Beth let her breath out slowly, silently, and then crawled the last few yards down the hall. Reaching the last door, she looked up and read the sign again. STUDENT RECORDS. She was there. She had made it.

Standing up slowly, Beth discovered that of all the doors along this hallway, this was the one that was fully closed, both top and bottom. She grasped the doorknob and turned it slowly.

The knob turned, the latch popped, and the door swung inward. Beth Picard slipped into the student records room, closing the door silently behind her.

CHAPTER 8

The first thing that struck Beth about the records room was the fact that the door had been unlocked. It worked out great for her, but why was it that anyone could just walk right in? The room had to contain detailed personal information about every student who had ever gone to Glenside. You'd think they would want to keep that info from falling into unauthorized hands.

Like hers.

The second thing that struck her about the room was how dark and crowded it was. It had the appearance of someone's closet in one of those TV shows about hoarders. The only light in the room was a thin band of sunlight that sliced through an otherwise filthy window and a strip of fluorescent light that crept in under the door.

Old oak file cabinets lined every wall, with another row of file cabinets running down the center of the narrow room. Beth wondered if there was enough space to fully open any of the drawers.

The room had a musty smell that reminded Beth of the used bookstore her mother enjoyed going to. Piles of green hanging folders and manila files were stacked on top of each cabinet. Cobwebs hung between the sides of the cabinets and the walls. A thick layer of dust seemed to cover everything as if it had been intentionally sprayed on like a coat of paint.

What a mess! Beth thought. *How can anyone find anything here? How will I find anything here?*

She glanced around, wondering where to begin. As with each step in this mission, she had no plan in place for what she would do when she reached it.

Somehow, through sheer luck it seemed, she had so far made it to the school, discovered a way in, slipped past the people working there, and found the door to the room she needed unlocked.

But now what? Where to start?

"Okay, first I need to find a light," Beth muttered softly to herself.

Searching for a light switch on the walls would be a waste of time, since she'd first have to search for the walls. Every available inch of wall space was covered by a cabinet or a shelf of some kind.

Miraculously Beth soon spotted a lamp. It was a classic table lamp with a brass base, a metal pull chain, and a green glass shade. She'd seen lamps like this in old movies. She pictured a grizzled old clerk sitting at a beat-up oak desk, counting coins by the dim glow of his green-shaded lamp.

Beth yanked the lamp's chain and the bulb sprang to life, casting a rectangular pool of light onto the low shelf on which it sat.

I guess I found my desk, she thought.

Beth tilted the lamp so that its light shone on the handwritten labels on the front of each file cabinet drawer. They were organized by months and years, though "organized" might be too strong a word to describe what she was looking at.

She scanned the various dates.

Let's see, Alice is in eighth grade now, and she said that Lizzie was in her grade. I'll start with the records three years ago and work my way forward.

Beth aimed the lamp's light at a lower drawer on a file cabinet. She grabbed a handful of files and opened the first one on the shelf near the lamp. Flipping through a stack of forms, each of which had a student's photo stapled to it, Beth waded through a sea of unfamiliar faces.

When she completed one folder, she moved on to the next one. As she finished each drawer, she opened the next and pulled out another stack of files, month by month, year by year.

Coming to the end of the third cabinet, Beth squeezed into the corner of the room to reach the next drawer in the chronological order she was following. Looking up, she realized that this drawer was the top one in a file cabinet resting on a platform. It was too tall for her to reach.

She stood on her tippy-toes and strained her shoulder trying to stretch her hand up to the drawer's handle, but she just could not reach. And even if she could manage to get the drawer open, how would she get the files out?

Standing in the corner next to this cabinet was a

ladder. *Is there even room enough in here to open this thing?* Beth wondered. There was only one way to find out.

Slowly and quietly Beth slipped the ladder from its resting place. Pulling the two hinged sections apart, she managed to pry it open. The legs on each side rested against the base of a file cabinet.

I just hope I can wriggle myself up and still be able to open that top drawer.

As Beth took her first step onto the ladder, she heard voices coming from the hallway just outside the door. She froze in place, on the bottom step, standing on one foot.

"This is the old student records room, huh?" said a woman with a young-sounding voice.

"Not so old," replied a man with a gruff voice. "It took this school a while to join the twenty-first century. Believe it or not, we only started keeping student records on computer this year."

"So what did you do before that?" asked the woman, sounding totally surprised. "Keep records on, like, paper?"

"Yup. Want to see? The door should be unlocked. Harold Wasser has been digitizing all the records in here so that we can eventually empty this room."

From her one-footed perch on the bottom step of the ladder Beth saw the doorknob turn and the door open slightly inward.

Fear coursed through her veins.

That's it. I'm finished, Beth thought. *My life is over. The school will have me arrested. My mom . . . I don't even want to think about my mom.*

"No time now," said the woman. "Got a meeting. Maybe later."

"Okay," said the man.

The door closed with a thud—the most beautiful sound Beth had ever heard.

When she heard the two sets of footsteps fade away, she stepped down off the ladder to compose herself, and also to give her aching left leg a rest.

Well that explains why the door was unlocked and why all these file folders are stacked on top of the cabinet, she thought in her relief. *Someone is taking all these paper records and scanning them into a computer.*

Beth started back up the ladder but then paused suddenly.

Which means that Harold Wasser could come in at any second to grab another handful of files!

Beth scrambled up with a new sense of urgency. She had to find what she needed and get out of there as soon as possible. Time was most definitely not her friend.

Reaching the highest step of the ladder, Beth slowly eased the drawer open and pulled out a fistful of folders. Placing them on top of the cabinet, she flipped through, page by page, searching for the face she knew all too well even by the dimmest of light.

About halfway through the first folder, Beth heard a noise. She paused. Glancing down, she saw a hand shoving the one tiny window in the room open. A face flashed in front of the window but vanished before Beth had a chance to process it.

Scrambling down the ladder, fretting the lost time in her search, Beth squeezed between two file cabinets and pressed herself against the window. She stuck her head out and caught a glimpse of a tall figure disappearing around a corner.

Elizabeth? Beth wondered at the retreating head of short, black hair.

Beth was confused, but she didn't have time to think much about what was going on. She would certainly get caught if she waited any longer. Not to mention that she needed to get home before her mom arrived.

She was halfway back up the ladder when she glimpsed more movement outside the window.

What now? she thought.

She climbed back down and peered out the window. Nothing, but then all of a sudden something popped up and grabbed her hand. Beth jumped back a bit before she noticed that it was only a curious black cat, on its hind legs, peering into the room. Beth reached out to pet the cat, but it hissed, then turned and bolted.

Beth wished she had more time to figure out what was going on, but she was in full-on panic mode now. She scrambled up the ladder and resumed her search. Finishing one folder, she riffled through the next, then another, then a fourth.

Last one, and then I have to get out of here, she thought.

Beth flipped open the green folder and there it was. After all the effort, all the nervousness, she saw it. Her own face stared up at her from the page. And there was the name:

Lizzie Maxwell.

Beth scanned the page with eager eyes. According to her file, Lizzie Maxwell lived a few blocks from the school, but that was about all there was to know about her in the records. Someone had scribbled a note on the page that she had stopped attending school in the middle of last year, a few weeks before Beth and her mom had moved to their new house.

Beth could review the page later. Right now she had to get out of there and return home. She stuck the page about Lizzie Maxwell back in the folder and tucked the folder under her arm.

I'll show these pages to Mom, she thought as she got ready to descend the ladder. *She'll finally have to tell me the truth. Is Lizzie my sister? My twin? Were we given up for adoption to two separate families when we were born? Mom got me and someone with the last name Maxwell got her? I have to know. I have to find—*

The ladder suddenly started shaking.

Whaa?

Beth glanced down and saw a tall young woman with dark hair. Her hand was on the ladder.

"Elizabeth? Why are you shaking the ladder? What are y—"

The door to the records room flew open, and a short man carrying a stack of file folders burst into the room.

"What on earth are you doing here?" the man shouted.

Beth was so startled she lost her balance, tumbled from the ladder, and crashed to the floor.

Beth looked up and saw the man bending over her, losing control of the files in his hands. File pages fluttered through the air, landing on top of Beth just before everything went black.

CHAPTER 9

Beep—beep—beep . . .

Beth awoke to a repetitive beeping sound.

Beep—beep—beep . . .

Forcing her eyes open, Beth saw that she was still sprawled out on the floor of the student records room. The file papers that had covered her were gone. So was the man who had burst into the room. She was alone again.

Beep—beep—beep . . .

But where was that sound coming from? It was driving her crazy!

Dragging herself up to her feet, Beth glanced around. Same overstuffed file cabinets. Same dim light. Same cramped, dusty room. So what was that beeping?

Beth walked slowly to the door.

What happened to that guy who found me here? she wondered. *Why did he just leave me on the floor? He cleaned up his precious papers but didn't get me any help? And was that Elizabeth shaking the ladder? Did she cause me to fall? But why would she do that? None of this makes any sense.*

Reaching the door, Beth turned the knob excruciatingly slowly so no one would hear her. When she felt the latch release, she opened the door just a crack and peeked out. What she saw made even less sense than the beeping sound.

Rather than leading back out to the hallway from which she had entered the records room, this door now opened into a laboratory. Not a science lab in a school, where students did experiments and worked on projects, but more like a mad scientist's lab from an old black-and-white horror movie, with bizarre and pointy medical instruments, tables piled with papers, and vials filled with liquids of all colors.

The mysterious lab appeared to be empty, or at least Beth couldn't hear anyone shuffling about. There was only one way to solve this mystery, and if there was one thing that Beth Picard had had enough of, it was mysteries.

She slowly stepped into the room.

Beep—beep—beep . . .

Maybe something in here is making the noise, Beth thought.

A series of lab tables sat in rows, and a large spotlight dangled above each one. The tables were cold and stark, bare except for a single thin white sheet on each one.

Lining the outer walls of the room were slate counters. Rising from each counter was a series of coiled glass tubes leading to round glass beakers that rested on the tables. Green, red, and blue liquids bubbled in the beakers; a rainbow mixture coursed through the coils.

"You have got to be kidding me," Beth muttered to herself. "It looks like they are filming *The Return of the Son of the Bride of Frankenstein's Mother-in-Law* or something like that. This can't be real."

Beep—beep—beep . . .

Beth continued to wander about the room. In the far corner sat a clear round glass tank full of milky liquid. Electrical cables snaked down from the ceiling and were attached to the sides of the tank. Every few seconds electric charges sparked through the water like lightning flashing through a dark night sky.

Beth approached the tank cautiously. She saw something floating in the murky liquid. It bobbed up to the surface, then sank again.

Beep—beep—beep . . .

Whatever was suspended in the liquid drifted to the surface again. This time it hovered for a moment, then spun around, revealing a tiny face. Ten miniscule fingers broke the surface next.

Beth jumped back from the edge of the tank in horror.

"It's a baby!" she cried, not caring who heard her at this point. "Why did someone put a baby in a tank of liquid? Is it alive?"

She moved back to the edge of the tank, and the baby sank out of view once again.

"Help!" she screamed, her strained voice echoing off the hard surfaces in the lab.

Someone touched Beth on the shoulder. She jumped into the air and spun around, all in one awkward motion.

When she landed, she found herself staring back at herself! Or maybe, just maybe, it was . . .

"Lizzie!" Beth cried. "Lizzie, I found you!"

She threw her arms around Lizzie, hugged her tightly.

And that's when Beth woke up only to find herself hugging a pillow, lying in a hospital bed.

Beep—beep—beep . . .

Beth took stock of her surroundings. She saw an IV dangling from her arm, leading to a machine . . . a machine that went *beep—beep—beep*.

"Try to relax, Beth," said a woman leaning over her. Beth didn't know the woman, but she guessed from her white coat and the stethoscope hanging around her neck, and the fact that she seemed to be in a hospital, that the woman was a doctor.

"Where am I?" Beth asked. "What happened? Who are you?"

"It's understandable that after an accident like the one you had, you'd be a little confused," the doctor said. "First thing's first. I'm Dr. Snow. I am in charge of your care here at North Side Hospital. As for what happened, you fell off a ladder at Glenside Middle School, bruised a rib, and hit your head on the floor. Fortunately, a teacher was in the room with you and he called an ambulance."

Oh, no! Beth thought. *Not another accident!*

As the memory of that afternoon flooded back to Beth, she realized that the laboratory, the floating baby, and the face-to-face with Lizzie were all just a dream. Another strange dream.

"Where's my mom?" Beth asked. She wanted her mother desperately, like a little kid who had just fallen off her bike and scraped her knee, but at the same time she was nervous for her mom's anger at disobeying the rules.

"I'm right here, honey!" called Beth's mom, throwing open the door and rushing into the room. "I got here as soon as I could."

She brushed past Dr. Snow, and Beth noticed that they exchanged a look that could only be described as uncomfortable. Beth also noticed that her mother looked sad, sadder than she'd ever seen her. Beth felt like bursting into tears. The last thing she had wanted to do was to upset her mother. She only wanted to know the truth.

"How are you feeling, sweetheart?" Beth's mom said gently, stroking Beth's hair.

Maybe I won't get in trouble for sneaking into the school after all, Beth thought hopefully.

"Everything's a little blurry," she replied. "It's hard to focus. My side hurts and my head hurts."

Beth rolled over. "Ow," she cried, grabbing her side. "I guess I really hurt my rib."

"More than just your rib, Beth," said Dr. Snow, handing her a small mirror. Beth turned her head to the side and looked in the mirror. She saw a reddish-purple lump pushing its way out through strands of her hair.

"That is a very nasty bump," replied Dr. Snow. "But all the scans indicated no severe head trauma, so I think Beth is one lucky young lady."

"I'm so relieved," said Beth's mom.

"What I'm wondering, of course, is what she was doing sneaking around a school she doesn't even go to?" Dr. Snow asked, her tone of voice a cross between contempt and disappointment. "I thought you homeschool Beth, Ms. Picard."

"I do!" Beth's mom shot back defensively. "I spend hours every day teaching Beth. I've devoted my life to her. I have been a strict and attentive parent!"

"Yet, somehow, not strict enough, apparently," Dr. Snow said softly, the impact of her words a stark contrast to the gentleness of her tone.

Beth stared up at the two women arguing over her. She knew she wasn't quite thinking clearly, but was the doctor actually arguing with her mom about what kind of parent she had been? Was this really the time and place for that kind of conversation?

"It appears to me," began Dr. Snow, "that it is time for this to come to an end."

"I want to speak with my daughter alone," Beth's mom said forcefully.

Dr. Snow turned and stormed out of the room without saying another word.

"What did she mean by that?" Beth asked when her mother had sat down on the edge of her bed. "'It is time for this to come to an end.'"

Beth's mom looked around the hospital room as if she was trying to avoid answering Beth's question. Finally, she spoke.

"She meant that the conversation we were having was over," Beth's mom explained. "Although she didn't have to be so rude about it."

"I thought the same thing," said Beth, shifting in her bed, trying to get more comfortable. "She was talking to you as if she knew you, and even then, it still would have been pretty rude."

"Her bedside manner does leave a lot to be desired, but

she is a good doctor—or at least that's what I've heard," said her mom. "You'll be in good hands with Dr. Snow, and anyway, we don't have much of a choice, do we?"

Beth nodded.

"But enough about her," her mom continued. "Do you want to explain what happened today?"

Beth sighed loudly. She knew that she would never have a better chance to tell her mom how she really felt. The sympathy factor of her being hurt was keeping her mom from getting really upset. It was now or never.

"I needed to know why I have no memories before this year," Beth began. "Meeting Chrissy, having a great friend like her, it all made it a little easier to forget that my life is a mystery to me."

Beth watched as tears welled up in her mother's eyes.

"But then I went to Chrissy's for that sleepover and everything changed," Beth continued. "I met Alice, who immediately thought I was someone named Lizzie. Alice claimed that she looked exactly like me. She was so sure of it, and I just couldn't let that thought go. Then Alice sent me that photo of Lizzie, and there was no denying it—she looked exactly like me.

"I searched every corner of the Internet but could

find nothing about Lizzie. Alice told me that she had met her at Glenside Middle School. I knew I had to go there. It was the only place where I could find out the truth."

Her mother shifted nervously on the bed.

"And, what did you find out?" she asked.

"I found her!" Beth exclaimed triumphantly. "Just before that man came into the records room, I found Lizzie's file. She's real. She did go to Glenside. And her picture was in the file. Front and center. She does look exactly like me!"

Her mother looked away.

"So, no more lies, Mom. When I get out of here, I'm going to find her. And I'll need your help," Beth continued. "Is she my sister? Why didn't you tell me about Lizzie?"

"I—I only wanted to protect you," Beth's mom said as the tears began to stream down her face.

"Protect me?" Beth asked in a sharper tone than she would have liked. "From what?"

The door to Beth's room swung open and Dr. Snow walked in, moving at a determined pace.

"I'm sorry," she said curtly, without a hint of sorrow

in her voice. "Visiting hours are over. Our patients need their rest."

Beth's mom stood up slowly.

"Mom, wait!" cried Beth. "What were you trying to protect me from?"

"I tried," her mom said, wiping the tears off her face. "I tried so hard to give you a normal life. And I did. This past year was wonderful. I'm glad we had it together."

"What do you mean?" asked Beth. "Of course you gave me a normal life. What are you talking about? And we'll have a lot more wonderful, normal years together too. I'm not dying. I just bumped my head."

"See you, honey. I love you," Beth's mom said sadly. Then she turned and hurried from the room.

Beth turned to face Dr. Snow. "What was that all about?

"I see it all the time," Dr. Snow replied. "Parents get very upset seeing their children in a hospital bed."

"I've never seen my mom so upset," Beth admitted. "How long do I have to stay here?"

"I want to keep you tonight, just to make sure your rib is healing properly and to make sure that bump on your head didn't shake you up more than it appears to have done," explained Dr. Snow. "You should go home tomorrow, but let's just play it one day at a time, okay?"

Dr. Snow smiled at Beth for the first time. Then she turned and left the room.

CHAPTER 10

Later that night Beth lay in her bed, in the dark, staring up at the stained ceiling tiles. The deep silence of the hospital was punctuated by occasional beeping or buzzing sounds, the ringing of phones, or soft footsteps padding down the hallway.

This is about the loneliest I think I've ever felt, thought Beth. *But that's not even the biggest part of it. I'm really missing Mom. It's like I just found out that she has to leave the country for a few years and is going to a place that has no phones or Internet.*

Yet it was just a feeling; her mother hadn't actually said good-bye, but Beth still felt this intense yearning for her mom.

Turning her head, she glanced over at the clock:

11:34 p.m. She tried to roll over onto her side, but a sharp, stabbing pain in her rib stopped her, sending her right over onto her back again.

The pain in her rib seemed to trigger a nagging pain in her skull, not really a headache, but a dull throbbing. She closed her eyes and tried to clear her mind. Finally, after what felt like hours, she drifted off into a fitful, restless sleep.

When her eyes reopened, the fog in her brain had cleared a bit. Beth looked at the clock again: 3:12 a.m. After a few more minutes of staring at the ceiling, Beth reached over and grabbed the controller that operated the bed. Pressing a button, she raised her head until she was in a sitting position, then turned on the light above her bed and grabbed a magazine from the small table beside her.

"If I can't sleep, I might as well read," she mumbled to herself, flipping the magazine open.

At this angle Beth could see past her propped-up knees to the other side of the room. On the opposite wall, near the door, a window looked out into the hallway. It was pretty busy outside her room during the day, but now, except for the occasional nurse walking by with a chart, it was empty.

As Beth mindlessly flipped through the pages of her magazine, something in the window caught her eye. There, standing in the hallway, looking into her room, was a girl who looked exactly like Beth.

"Lizzie?" Beth wondered aloud. "Lizzie!"

Fighting past the pain, Beth tossed her magazine aside and threw off the covers. She struggled out of bed, wincing and moaning. Stumbling to the window, she pressed her face against the glass and felt as if she were looking in the mirror. Then suddenly Lizzie bolted.

Walking with great difficulty, her rib now burning from the pain, Beth shuffled to the door and threw it open. She stepped out into the hall and looked in both directions, but there was no sign of Lizzie.

Wait a minute! Beth thought, struggling back into her room. She glanced over at her bed, half expecting to see herself lying there. *How many dreams have I had lately in which I saw a girl, or lots of girls, who looked like me? Could this be another one?*

She reached her bed and crawled back in.

If this is a dream, it's pretty cruel that I would dream myself in so much pain! Still, what sense does it make that after all I've gone through to find her, Lizzie just shows up here at my hospital room at three o'clock in the morning!

Exhausted by the act of walking across her room, and emotionally drained from the events of the past twenty-four hours, Beth finally drifted off into a deep sleep.

She had no dreams for the rest of the night—at least none that she could remember.

Dr. Snow entered Beth's room early the next morning, clutching a new set of X-rays that had been taken late the previous day. She flipped on the light above Beth's bed, startling her out of her slumber.

"Sorry for the rude awakening, Beth," Dr. Snow said, "but things get going pretty early around here. And I wanted to discuss these X-rays with you."

Grimacing with pain, Beth sat up in the bed so she could get a better look. Dr. Snow held the X-rays up against a light box.

"Now, you see this dark line right here," Dr. Snow said, pointing to a spot on the film. "That's the bruise on your rib. Unfortunately it's worse than we first thought.

I'm afraid I'm going to have to keep you in the hospital for at least one more night."

Beth slumped down in disappointment, although a part of her was relieved. With as much pain as she was in, she knew that she'd be more comfortable here, though she was anxious to get back home to her mother after the weird way she had left the previous day.

"Dr. Snow, this may sound like a strange question, but is there another patient in the hospital who looks like me?" Beth asked.

Dr. Snow smiled. "Why do you ask?"

"Last night I saw a girl who looked exactly like me standing out in the hallway, staring at me through that window," Beth replied, pointing to the window on the far wall.

"No, no one who looks like you that I know of," Dr. Snow said. "But it's not unusual to have very vivid dreams in a hospital, especially dreams about missing your friends or kids your own age."

Beth nodded. She decided not to tell Dr. Snow about all the other dreams she'd been having lately in which she saw girls who looked like her.

"Speaking of kids your own age," Dr. Snow continued,

"my daughter is here with me at the hospital today. She's about your age. It's gotta be pretty boring lying around here by yourself. Maybe she can stop by a little later and you two can hang out. It might help break up the boredom."

"That sounds like a great idea," said Beth. She smiled at Dr. Snow. "Thanks."

"Great, I'll let her know," said Dr. Snow. "Now I've got to check in on my other patients." She turned and left the room.

Beth spent the next hour or so reviewing the events of the past few days. She pondered what she might have done differently and couldn't really come up with anything. She thought about her mom and how strangely she had acted yesterday.

Beth's ruminations were interrupted by a knock on her door.

"Come in," she called out.

The door swung open and in walked a girl. Beth couldn't see her clearly at first in the harsh, cold fluorescent light of the hospital room. The girl was tall. She appeared to have short black hair and pale skin.

"Hi!" the girl said, stepping into the room, her head

down so her hair covered her face. "I'm Elizabeth. I'm Dr. Snow's daughter. She told me that you might like some company."

"Sure," said Beth. "Thanks. I'm Beth."

"I know," said Elizabeth, coming closer to the bed and lifting her head.

Beth was stunned to discover that the girl in her room was indeed Elizabeth—the same Elizabeth whom Beth had met yesterday. The same Elizabeth who went to Glenside Middle School and helped Beth sneak inside.

But what in the world was she doing here?

CHAPTER 11

"Elizabeth!" Beth cried. "I can't believe it!"

But Beth's happiness didn't last for long. She suddenly remembered seeing Elizabeth at the window in the records room, shaking the ladder just before the man came into the room and Beth fell.

"What happened in the records room?" she asked. "I remember seeing you just before I fell."

"I was trying to stop you from getting caught," Elizabeth explained. "As I was on my way out of the school, I overheard a conversation about how the school was in the process of scanning all the old records, and how someone would be in and out of the room all day."

Beth recalled the conversation she had heard through the door about Harold Wasser.

"I didn't want to risk going back into the building and getting caught," Elizabeth continued, "so I went around to the window, hoping I could climb in. But the opening was too small."

"But why didn't you just talk to me through the open window?" Beth asked. "You could have warned me."

"Just as I was about to do that I heard someone coming," Elizabeth replied. "I got scared and ran away."

In her mind, Beth went through the series of events that had happened in the records room. Things remained a bit fuzzy for her, but what Elizabeth just explained made sense.

"And now here you are," Beth said.

"Here I am," Elizabeth repeated. "I think there's a ladder out in the hall you can climb on if you like. You know, for old times' sake!"

Beth started to laugh. Elizabeth joined her. Beth realized that this was the biggest, most genuine laugh she had had since the night of the sleepover at Chrissy's. She was surprised by how immediately comfortable she felt with Elizabeth, as if she had known her for her entire life.

And she also realized that laughing made her rib hurt. She winced and clutched her side.

"Are you in a lot of pain?" asked Elizabeth.

"Only when I laugh, doctor," replied Beth, sending them both into gales of laughter once again.

"Shhh," cautioned Elizabeth, putting a finger to her lips. "We'll disturb the other patients."

"Not to mention my poor rib!" said Beth.

And again the two girls laughed loudly.

"So, " Elizabeth began when the laughter subsided, "did you find that girl? What was her name—Wait, don't tell me. Lizzie, right?"

"Yes, Lizzie, and yes, I found her!" Beth said triumphantly.

Elizabeth gave her a high five.

"Well, I didn't find *her*, of course," Beth continued. "I haven't been anywhere but the hospital since I saw you, but I did find the file about her."

"And?" asked Elizabeth.

"And I was right!" said Beth. "Or I should say my friend Chrissy's cousin Alice was right. Lizzie did go to

Glenside and she did look like me. I mean, *exactly* like me, like a twin sister."

"So what are you going to do?" Elizabeth asked. "How are you going to find her?"

"I don't know," answered Beth honestly. "One second I was thrilled to have found her file, and the next second I was falling off a ladder, blacking out, and waking up here."

"Well, you should stay here and get well and worry about Lizzie later," said Elizabeth.

Beth nodded. "That's the plan. Dr. Snow—your mom—told me I would have to stay here at least one more night."

"Well then, let's make the best of it!" cried Elizabeth. She pulled out her phone. "I have thirty-eight games on here. My favorite, though, is Counting Chickens. I'll show you how it works. It's easy!"

It only took a few minutes for Beth to get the hang of the game. When they got tired of playing Counting Chickens, they moved on to another game. The minutes melted away. At times Beth even forgot that she was in a hospital bed; she was so focused on playing with Elizabeth.

"I see you two are getting along well," Dr. Snow observed, walking into the room.

"Elizabeth's awesome, Dr. Snow," said Beth. "Thanks for bringing her here."

"Well, I think Elizabeth thinks you're pretty awesome too," Dr. Snow said. "Because of my schedule, and how much time I spend here, she has to be here a lot, so I'm glad she found a friend."

Dr. Snow listened to Beth's heartbeat, took her blood pressure and temperature, then felt around her rib, being careful not to press too hard.

"You seem to be healing nicely, Beth," she said. "You'll spend the night and then we'll reevaluate tomorrow. Now don't let me interrupt your fun any longer. I think you two are going to be great friends!"

"Thanks, Mom!" said Elizabeth.

"Yeah, thanks, Dr. Snow, for taking such good care of me," said Beth.

Dr. Snow smiled and left the room.

"Now, where were we?" Elizabeth asked. "Oh, yeah, level nine of Cosmic Climb. It's your turn. You're on the Labyrinth Ladders. You have to make it to the Vanishing Vault before the Dark Demons finish you off. Ready?"

"Ready!"

"Resume!"

The two girls played all the way through the afternoon, pausing only to eat. Over lunch, Beth grew curious about her new acquaintance.

"So, do you have a lot of friends?" she asked Elizabeth between bites of her tuna sandwich.

"Not many," Elizabeth replied, her shoulders slumping, her eyes looking away. "Most of the friends I've ever had have left. They're not here anymore. I get lonely sometimes." Then her face brightened. "That's why I'm glad I met you."

"Me too," said Beth. "I don't have many friends either. Just Chrissy, my neighbor. It's nice to have a new friend."

Elizabeth gave Beth a gentle hug, being careful not to squeeze too hard. "I'm so glad to hear you say that."

Beth smiled. "Now all I have to do is get well and get out of this hospital."

Elizabeth smiled back but didn't say anything.

"So, what's our next game?" asked Beth.

"Journey through the Elf Kingdom," said Elizabeth. "You get to be a queen, or a ghost warrior, or a sorcerer princess. You have to journey through the kingdom to get to the Golden Palace of the Elves before the Crazy Creatures get you."

"Cool," said Beth, unable to remember the last time she'd had so much fun. "I'll be a sorcerer princess."

"I'll be a ghost warrior," said Elizabeth. "Let the game begin!"

The girls battled trolls, recited secret chants, unfurled ancient spells, and trekked through stormy forests and over craggy mountains until they finally reached the Golden Palace of the Elves.

Beth completely lost track of time. She was surprised when the tray with her dinner arrived and Elizabeth had to leave.

"Will I see you tomorrow?" Beth asked anxiously.

"Of course," said Elizabeth, smiling broadly. "We've got twenty-one more games to get through!"

"Thanks," said Beth. "This was a really great day."

"I think we're going to have lots more great days for a long time!" said Elizabeth. "See ya tomorrow."

Beth ate her dinner, watched a little TV, then drifted off to sleep. She had had so much fun with Elizabeth that it never even occurred to her that her mother hadn't come to visit that day.

CHAPTER 12

That night Beth slept deeply, dreamlessly, until something woke her up. It sounded like a distant voice calling to her, penetrating her sleep. As her mind cleared slightly, she realized where she was. She looked at the clock: 12:44 a.m. Then she discovered the source of the voice.

Sitting up, Beth could clearly hear two people yelling. They seemed to be right outside her room. She climbed carefully from her bed, threw on her robe and slippers, and went to the window that looked out into the hallway. She was stunned by what she saw.

There, standing in the hallway, was Dr. Snow. She was arguing with a girl who appeared, despite all logic to the contrary, to be Lizzie!

Beth froze. She desperately wanted to rush out into the hall, talk to Lizzie, and confirm once and for all that she was not crazy, that she truly did have a twin sister. But something held her back. She was intimidated by Dr. Snow and didn't want to interrupt her or get in trouble for butting in where she didn't belong.

Beth watched as an attendant rushed over to Lizzie, gently but firmly pulled her away from Dr. Snow, and led her down the hall. As Dr. Snow composed herself after an argument that had clearly shaken her, she glanced toward the window and caught Beth's eye.

Beth gasped and hurried back toward her bed.

Dr. Snow walked into the room.

"Are you all right, Beth?" Dr. Snow asked, as if nothing unusual had just happened. "What are you doing out of bed so late?"

"I was awakened by the yelling," Beth blurted out.

"Yelling?" Dr. Snow said, sounding very surprised. "What do you mean?"

"Just now. Out in the hall. You and Lizzie were arguing."

"Lizzie? Who's Lizzie?" Dr. Snow asked.

"That girl you were fighting with in the hallway," Beth

explained, stunned and a little annoyed that Dr. Snow was acting as if she had no idea what Beth was talking about. "You know, the girl who looks *exactly* like me!"

"I don't know what you mean," said Dr. Snow in her most calm, professional tone. "I was just making my late-night rounds, looking in on some of the more critically ill patients."

"I'm sorry, Dr. Snow," Beth began, unable to disguise how upset she was. "Are you saying that you were not arguing with a girl in the hall just now? That I imagined all that? I'm obviously not dreaming, since I'm here talking to you."

"Now, calm down, Beth," said Dr. Snow, reaching into the pocket of her long, white coat and pulling out a syringe. "Sometimes patients can go a little loopy in the hospital. The technical term is 'hospital psychosis.' They have weird dreams that they think are real, or imagine seeing things that didn't really happen."

"That's not what this is!" Beth insisted.

"You're getting a little agitated, Beth," said Dr. Snow. "I'm going to give you a little something to help you sleep. You'll feel better and see things more clearly after a good night's sleep."

Before Beth could protest, Dr. Snow stuck a needle into her arm and gave her a shot.

Beth instantly felt drowsy. Dr. Snow helped her get back into bed. Beth mumbled something about Lizzie and then fell into a very deep sleep.

Beth opened her eyes slowly. She felt rested, better rested in fact than she had felt in a long time. Yawning, she stretched her arms and felt a pinch of pain up near her left shoulder.

The shot! Dr. Snow gave me a shot to help me sleep!

Memories of last night flooded back—the argument in the hall, seeing Lizzie, Dr. Snow denying that Beth had seen anything. It was all so very strange.

And that's when Beth noticed that she had been moved to a different room. This room looked much more like a girl's room in a house than a hospital room.

I must have really been out last night, Beth thought. *But why was I moved? And where am I? Am I still in the hospital?*

Looking around, Beth saw a second bed, covered by a pink bedspread with fuzzy pom-poms and tassels dangling off the edges. A shelf filled with dolls sat across from the bed. A small vanity with a mirror held makeup and hairbrushes. A guitar sat on a stand in the corner.

One whole side of the room was covered by curtains. Beth climbed out of her bed and pulled the cord that opened the curtains. They parted, revealing a wall with six photos. Each photo was of a girl who looked exactly like Beth, with her auburn hair and freckles. At first Beth thought each was a different photo of the same girl, but then she noticed the labels. Under each photo was a number and the name of a different girl. In order from one to six they read: Liza, Betty, Bess, Liz, Lizzie . . . and Beth.

Beth gaped at the pictures as she tried to grasp at their meaning. It was more like looking into a series of mirrors than photos. The pictures made her think of all the dreams she'd had recently involving mirrors and multiple images of herself.

Baffled and curious, Beth reached out and touched the first photo.

Suddenly Beth's mind flooded with images— memories and experiences that felt as if they had happened to her, vivid feelings, smells, strong memories.

She was at a beach. She could feel the wind whipping

through her hair, smell the salt water and French fries, hear the sound of a baseball game coming out of a nearby radio and waves crashing against the shore.

She let go of the photo and was instantly back in the room, stunned and a bit out of breath.

What was that? she wondered, at once fascinated and terrified. Her curiosity quickly overcame her fear. Beth reached out and touched the next photo. Again she was overwhelmed by a flood of memories.

This time she was riding a mountain bike down a twisting, bumpy dirt road that wrapped around the side of a steep mountain. She felt the wind in her face and the sensation of extremely fast movement coupled with a palpable sense of danger.

Suddenly Beth saw another rider out of the corner of her eye, drifting toward her, edging her closer to the cliff side of the bike path.

"Look out!" she cried, not completely sure whether she had actually screamed or just screamed in the vision in her head. But either way she found herself bouncing and rolling toward the cliff.

The other bike came closer, pushing Beth right over the edge. She tumbled toward a canyon below—

—and yanked her hand from the photo with such force that she stumbled backward and fell.

So real, she thought. *What kind of power do these pictures have?*

Fighting the pain in her rib, Beth climbed back onto her feet and touched the third photo.

Her mind spun in confusion. Nothing made sense. She couldn't put a coherent thought together. Then everything went black as if she had suddenly lost her vision. She stumbled helplessly, banging into walls and crashing into furniture. She quickly let go of the photo and returned to the room she was in.

There was something so exhilarating about this exercise that despite the unpleasant memories some of the photos contained, Beth felt compelled to touch each one.

She touched the fourth photo and her mind went almost completely blank. She stared at the wallpaper in a tiny room and began counting the flowers in the pattern. When she reached one hundred, she started again.

Beth took her hand off picture number four and touched picture number five. She found herself in a crowded, noisy school cafeteria. Looking up, she spotted a banner for the school basketball team. It read: "Go Glenside Tigers!"

Beth was stunned that for some reason she was experiencing a memory of going to Glenside Middle School.

That's when a tall, skinny girl with long, straight brown hair stepped up to her.

"Hey, Lizzie," said the girl. "Do you want to eat lunch with me today?"

Beth looked up and recognized the girl as Alice, Chrissy's cousin, the one who went to Glenside, who thought that Beth looked like some girl named Lizzie, the Lizzie whose memory Beth was now obviously experiencing.

She let go of the photo, trying desperately to put the pieces together. It still all made no sense.

One more photo. No point in stopping now.

She touched the sixth photo. Nothing happened. She took her finger away, then touched the photo again. Still nothing.

Why doesn't this one trigger any memories? she wondered.

"That one's you," said a familiar voice coming from behind her.

Beth spun around and saw Elizabeth.

"Elizabeth!" Beth cried, throwing her arms around her friend. "I am so glad to see you!"

"I planned to be here when you woke up," Elizabeth said. "Sorry about that."

"Where am I?" asked Beth.

"My room," Elizabeth replied simply.

"What do you mean, your room?" Beth asked. "Are we still in the hospital? This doesn't look like a hospital room."

Elizabeth smiled. "This is a special room in the hospital that my mom set up for me," she explained. "She spends so much time here that she wanted me to be able to stay over and still feel like I had my own space. My mom suggested moving you in here because she thought that you would be more comfortable, since you and I get along so well."

Beth was about to ask Elizabeth about the photos, but Elizabeth wasn't finished. "Listen, Beth, I want to apologize. I'm really sorry that fight between me and my mom woke you up last night. I really wish you hadn't seen that."

"What are you talking about?" said Beth. "I didn't

see you. I saw someone who looks exactly like *me*."

Elizabeth smiled and lifted her hand up to her head. In one swift motion she pulled a black wig off. A mane of auburn hair tumbled down around her shoulders. She pulled a washcloth from a drawer in her vanity and wiped the pale makeup off her face, revealing freckles, tons of them, just like Beth had. Then she kicked off the high platform shoes she'd been wearing and put on a pair of slippers, making her exactly the same height as Beth.

And for about the millionth time since this whole craziness began, Beth found herself staring at someone who looked exactly like her.

"Lizzie?" gasped Beth.

"No. It's still me . . . Elizabeth," Elizabeth answered. "And that was me you saw last night, Beth. And the night before. And yes, I look exactly like you! Or, to be perfectly accurate, you look exactly like me!"

CHAPTER 13

Beth stumbled back, away from Elizabeth. She bumped into the side of the bed and sat down. Her head was spinning.

"I—I don't understand," she mumbled. "What's going on?"

"It's time you knew everything," said Elizabeth. "Especially now that you have seen and experienced the photos." She gestured toward the wall of photos.

"About twenty-five years ago my mother performed an experiment on me," Elizabeth began.

"Wait! Twenty-five years ago?" said Beth, completely bewildered. "But you're my age!"

"Just listen," Elizabeth said softly. "It will all make

sense in a moment. You see, although my mom is a really good doctor, she has a bit of mad scientist in her too.

"Twenty-five years ago, when I was twelve, my mom performed an experiment on me that she hoped would increase my intelligence. It didn't. Instead it froze the growth mechanisms in my body at the cellular level."

"What?" asked Beth, trying desperately but failing miserably to comprehend what she was hearing.

"I became permanently twelve," answered Elizabeth. "And I would remain twelve years old for as long as I lived. Now, at first I didn't mind the idea of being a kid forever. But as my friends all grew up and moved on with their lives, I didn't. I stayed the same."

Beth recalled what Elizabeth had said over lunch the day before: *Most of the friends I've ever had have left. They're not here anymore. I get lonely sometimes.*

Elizabeth continued: "So then, about twenty years ago, my mother tried to give me a gift to make up for what she had done to me. She created a clone using my DNA. Since my DNA had been permanently altered to stop me from aging, the clone was twelve years old—and, like me, would stay that way forever.

"And because the clone was made from my DNA,

it had my memories embedded in its genetic structure. These memories were deep, hidden beneath the surface of everyday awareness, but they were there."

"That explains a lot," Beth said, thinking back to the dream she had the night before she headed to Glenside. She had wondered how she could have such vivid memories of a childhood she had no real recollection of and never really experienced.

"Clone number one was Liza, and we had lots of fun together. But one day at the beach, she escaped. I guess she got tired of spending all her time with me and wanted to move on with her life, but she had no idea that she couldn't. She would always remain the same. She's probably still wandering around out there somewhere, alone, unable to grow up."

Beth's brain was having trouble processing all this, yet one word jumped out and gnawed at her: "escaped."

Had Liza been held captive against her will? Beth wondered.

Elizabeth continued. "Clone number two, Betty, had what we'll just call a biking accident. Sad, but fortunately clone number three, Bess, was right there to take her place. But it turned out that number three was defective, so I got rid of her."

Got rid of her! thought Beth. *How? What does that mean?*

"Number four, Liz, was just too boring, so I got rid of her, too," said Elizabeth.

Suddenly Beth understood what she had seen when she touched the photographs a few minutes ago. Number four had been boring, just counting numbers in her head all day. Number two had had a bike accident. When she touched the photos, she experienced their memories.

"And clone number five was Lizzie," said Beth, the whole crazy picture finally coming into sharp focus. "The Lizzie I've been searching for. I saw her in Glenside when I touched her picture just now."

"Yup," said Elizabeth. "She ran away from me too. Just a few weeks ago. Which brings us to clone number six."

"Me," Beth said. "I'm number six. You gave each clone a nickname based on your name—Elizabeth."

"Good thinking, Beth," said Elizabeth. "You're a smart one. We're going to get along great."

"And that's why nothing happened when I touched the sixth picture," said Beth. "Because it is of me. Instead of seeing through someone else's eyes, I just saw my own experience, which at that moment was simply me touching that picture."

"Yes," said Elizabeth. "And because some of the clones ran away, I asked my mother to do something special for number six. My mom and her assistant implanted a homing chip in *your* body so that I could find you if you ever escaped."

"So it was no accident that you tracked me down and ran into me that day near Glenside," said Beth, feeling the skin on her arm for a chip. "You tracked me, and followed me to the school so we would meet. You needed a new friend."

"Yes," answered Elizabeth. "Your 'mother,' Nancy Picard, was proving difficult. She was supposed to take care of you until I had need of you, but when the time came, she didn't want to give you back. I wasn't sure how I was going to get you, but you made it so easy when you went off that day by yourself. It was only a matter of getting you to the hospital and under my mother's care. It was me who shook the ladder that day and caused you to fall."

Beth grew frightened. She wondered how far Elizabeth would go to get what she wanted.

"But I still don't understand why I don't have any memories," remarked Beth.

Elizabeth nodded. "When you were created, you were twelve years old. Any memories you had from the time you were 'born' in the lab to the time my mother's assistant took you away for safekeeping were erased with a drug. Until I needed you, you would have no idea who you were or where you came from."

"My mom was your mom's assistant!" Beth said, the whole terrible truth dawning on her.

"Yes, your mom was, and still is, a brilliant research scientist," Elizabeth explained. "She worked closely with my mom on developing and refining the clones. When she agreed to take you home for safekeeping, she signed a contract saying that she would return you when the time came."

"So the day we moved into the new house was the day she brought me home from the lab," said Beth.

Beth hugged herself tightly. She no longer cared about the pain in her rib. Everything she knew about her life was wrong. She now understood why her mother had acted so strangely the other day when she left. She knew that she would never see Beth again, that Beth now belonged to Elizabeth, and like Elizabeth she would never grow any older.

Of course she had no memories of her childhood. She had never had a childhood. She came into existence at twelve and would always be that age.

Elizabeth put her arm around Beth.

"Will you be my friend?" Elizabeth asked.

Beth wanted to run, to flee the building, to get away and never come back. But because of her homing chip, she knew that Elizabeth would find her, maybe even "get rid of her."

"S-sure," said Beth. "I'll be your friend."

"Great!" said Elizabeth, smiling brightly and pulling her phone out of her pocket. "We've got twenty-one more games to get through and all the time in the world to play them!"

EPILOGUE

FIVE YEARS LATER . . .

"What do you mean you're bored, Elizabeth?" Beth asked as the two girls walked through a park.

"Don't get upset, Beth," said Elizabeth. "It's been great fun having you as my friend for the past five years. It's been so cool living like twin sisters, which we are, in a futuristic sort of way."

"Strange" would be the word I would use, rather than "cool," Beth thought. But as usual, she kept her thoughts to herself.

It had taken Beth a few years, but she had finally gotten used to watching other people grow up and get older while she and Elizabeth remained forever twelve years old.

They did have fun together, but for all intents and purposes Beth was a prisoner, unable to leave or come and go as she pleased, and that fact was never far from the front of her mind.

"I just think that having another friend to hang out with us would be great," explained Elizabeth.

"But what happens when the new friend grows up and we don't?" Beth asked. "Sooner or later, anyone else is going to outgrow us."

"Not a problem," said Elizabeth.

A wave of fear shot through Beth.

Oh, no. She's talking about another clone, about Elizabeth number seven. What if she's planning to get rid of me like she did some of the others?

The pair approached the hospital. They had been sharing Elizabeth's room there for the past five years. Beth had started to think of the place as home, although she missed the house that she had once lived in with a woman she called "Mom." She missed Nancy Picard, whom she had not seen since that day at the hospital, right after her fall from the ladder.

Once inside, Beth and Elizabeth made their way

toward their room. Elizabeth reached out and grabbed the doorknob.

"Ready to meet our new friend?" she asked.

Ready as I'll ever be, Beth thought. She simply nodded.

Elizabeth opened the door and the two girls stepped into the room. Standing inside was a girl who looked to be about seventeen.

Beth stared at her. There was something so familiar about this girl. Beth was certain that they had met.

"Beth, meet Tina," said Elizabeth. "Tina, this is Beth."

Tina had short blond hair and two different-colored eyes, one blue and one hazel.

"Chrissy?" Beth asked in shock. "Is that you?"

Beth had not seen Chrissy since the day she left to go to Glenside. Five years had passed, so this girl would be the right age.

"Um, maybe you have me confused with someone else?" the girl said. "My name is Tina, short for Christina."

"Give us a second, Tina," Elizabeth asked.

"Sure," Tina replied.

Elizabeth pulled Beth out into the hallway.

"Chrissy!" Beth cried. "You kidnapped Chrissy!"

"Slow down, Beth," said Elizabeth. "Nobody

kidnapped anyone. That's not Chrissy, that's Tina. And I thought you'd be pleased, since she looks so much like your old best friend."

Slowly the truth dawned on Beth.

"A clone," she whispered. "Tina is Chrissy's clone!"

"Exactly," replied Elizabeth, smiling. "When I told my mom that I was bored with just having you for a friend, she agreed to make me a new one. But rather than another clone of me, I thought we could clone someone that would make *you* happy—Chrissy."

"But why didn't she recognize me?" Beth wondered.

"Well, just like with all the other clones, my mom gave her a drug that erased all her memories before the point of cloning. Of course she's aged a bit, but she's still a clone of your best friend. And now the three of us will be great friends. Come on! Let's go get to know her. I'll bet you'll come to like her as much as you liked Chrissy." With that, Elizabeth bounced back into the room.

Beth sighed as she followed Elizabeth. She had no choice but to follow. She was glad that she wasn't going to be eliminated, but she was as sad as always. She would never know how long her waking nightmare would last. Her best guess was forever.

DO NOT FEAR—
WE HAVE ANOTHER CREEPY TALE FOR YOU!

TURN THE PAGE FOR A SNEAK PEEK AT

You're invited to a

CREEPOVER®

Don't Move a Muscle

The middle school bus came so early in the morning, and took so long getting to school, that one of Cora Nicolaides's parents usually drove her and picked her up. Her dad was working from home today, so it would be his turn for pickup that afternoon. Cora took her time as she walked to the carpool section of the parking lot after school. Her dad was usually a little late, and besides, she was deep in thought. It wasn't the dance that was on her mind this time—or at least not the actual dance. It was a problem from her math class. Her math teacher, Mr. Ferris, always made a big deal about how helpful math could be in real life. That afternoon he had come up with a problem that was obviously meant to be "timely."

The Dance Committee is setting up square tables for the eighth-grade dance. Each table seats four, and the committee may use as many tables as it needs. Tables may be pushed together, but no table arrangement may seat more than twelve. (Why? Because Mr. Ferris says so.) Show three different ways that sixteen couples could be seated for the dance.

Cora wished Mr. Ferris had written "thirty-two people" instead of "sixteen couples," but this was the kind of math question she liked. She was walking slowly along, staring at the ground and imagining different table arrangements, when someone suddenly crashed into her.

"Whoa! Sorry! I didn't see you."

Startled, Cora looked up at the boy who had just bumped into her. He was a little older than she was and incredibly handsome. He had dark, wavy hair, an olive complexion, and eyes that were almost black. He was several inches taller than Cora, and he was smiling down at her. His smile was pretty incredible too.

"I—I'm the one who should be sorry," Cora stammered. "I was thinking about a math problem."

"And I was going too fast," said the boy. "Tell you what. We can both be sorry. How does that sound?"

Cora smiled shyly back at him. "Sounds good."

"I guess I just proved that haste really does make waste," said the boy. "Wait—that didn't come out right. It's never a waste to bump into a cute girl."

Cora could feel herself blushing.

"But," he continued, "I did drop all these postcards I'm supposed to be rushing to the post office."

Now Cora saw that a pile of cards was scattered all over the ground. "Let me help!" she said. "Seeing as I'm so sorry and all."

"Thanks—that'd be great. By the way, my name is Evan."

"I'm Cora. Do you go to school here?"

Evan was down on his knees scrambling to pick up the postcards. He stopped for a second to gesture toward the high school across the parking lot and the football field beyond it. "Yup, right over there. I'm a freshman. I'm on my way to work."

"Work?"

Evan laughed. "Well, 'work' sounds better than 'after-school job,' don't you think?"

He was already on his feet and reaching out for the few postcards Cora picked up. She handed them over reluctantly. If only there had been a lot more postcards so that Evan could have stayed longer! But it wasn't going to happen. He'd gotten all the cards back in order much too quickly.

"Gotta run—I'm already late," he said. "See you around." In a few seconds he had turned the corner and disappeared from sight.

Wistfully Cora watched him go. She had just had an actual conversation with a high school boy! Unfortunately, she would probably never see him again. . . .

"*Who* was *that*? He's *cute*." Hailey had come up from behind without Cora even noticing.

"He's definitely cute," Cora agreed. "His name is Evan. He's a freshman. He has a job after school. And that's probably all I'll ever know about him."

"I know one more thing. He missed that card." When Hailey pointed, Cora realized that one of Evan's postcards was lying at her feet. She picked it up and looked at it more closely. The picture side had a black-and-white photo showing a cluster of statues on a lawn somewhere. Along the bottom were the words METAXAS SCULPTURE GARDEN INVITES YOU. . . .

"Invites us to what?" said Cora. She flipped the card over. "'Please come to the unveiling of our newest acquisition,'" she read aloud. "Oh—it's the day after the dance."

"What's an acquisition?" asked Hailey.

"I think that's what museums call it when they buy a work of art," answered Cora.

"You can't invite someone to a work of art!"

"No," said Cora, "but you can invite them to come see it. The statue must be covered up, or something, and people can come watch them uncover it."

But Hailey didn't seem interested in that part of the story. "It's like Cinderella in reverse!" she said now. "The prince dropped his postcard when he ran away. Don't you want to track him down so you can give it back?"

Cora shook her head. "He's probably a mile away by now. And it's just one postcard. He won't miss it." Carefully she tucked the card between two books in her backpack so that it wouldn't get bent.

Hailey gave a fake-romantic sigh. "Your only souvenir of the mysterious Evan."

"Oh, stop," said Cora. She was relieved to see her dad's car pulling up. She waved at him, then turned to Hailey. "Want a ride home?"

When the two girls had arranged themselves in the

back seat and Cora's father had pulled out of the parking lot, Hailey said, "Okay. So. How did you meet cute, cute Evan?"

Cora gave her a quick explanation, and Hailey nodded in a satisfied way. "Very romantic."

"Is this guy someone I should know about?" asked Cora's father, glancing at Cora in the rearview mirror.

"*Dad!* No! I'm sure I'll never see him again," said Cora.

"He must work at the sculpture garden," suggested Hailey. "It's pretty close by. Have you ever been there?"

"No. I've only heard the name."

Hailey, who was never shy about asking for favors, leaned forward in her seat. "Mr. Nicolaides, could you drive us past the sculpture garden? Your uneducated daughter has never seen it before."

"Guess I've failed as a parent," said Cora's dad. "Well, it's easy to fix. Sure, I'll take us over that way."

The garden was on the corner of a quiet street a few blocks from the girls' school. The house, a dark red Victorian, was tucked back from the road. Stone paths led to the front door and, from a side door, into the sculpture garden.

Nothing about the house should have been unsettling.

It should have looked like the cozy nest it had been built to be. But instead it looked forlorn and neglected. The dark, shaggy shrubs in front hadn't been trimmed in ages. Inside, Cora could see that curtains had been drawn across every window on both floors.

The garden didn't look very welcoming either. Cora hadn't been quite sure what a sculpture garden was. This was nothing like she'd imagined. The lot was enclosed by an ornate wrought-iron fence that made the statues look like prisoners. Stunted trees had been placed here and there. Apart from them, there was also a tall rectangular hedge—a labyrinth, Hailey said.

The statues she could see from the road had been arranged in clusters. They'd been carved out of some kind of grayish stone and made to look like gods, goddesses, and heroes, though here and there Cora spied a few ordinary people throughout different periods in history. They were very realistic. For some reason, Cora didn't enjoy looking at them.

She shuddered a little. "Kind of creepy," she said.

"*Totally* creepy," said Hailey emphatically. "When I was about five, my parents took me here. I don't remember it too well, but my mom says I completely freaked out—they had to take me home. What I don't understand is how anyone could *collect* statues like these."

"There have always been rumors about this place," said Cora's father. "Statues coming to life, strange goings-on in the museum—things like that. All urban legends, but still spooky. Anyway, have you looked at this long enough?"

"Yes!" said both girls in unison.

As Mr. Nicolaides began to drive away from the curb, a branch on one of the nearby trees suddenly shifted position—or at least that was how it looked. Most likely, it was the wind. But Cora had the unmistakable impression that an unseen hand had shoved the branch away.

The branch had been concealing the face of the nearest statue. And the expression on the statue's face was terrible.

It was the figure of a woman. She was wearing a tight-fitting buttoned jacket and what looked like a hoopskirt from the nineteenth century. The clothes had been carved with such amazing skill that the long stone skirt actually seemed to be rippling like fabric. Her hands were covering her eyes to shield them from . . . what?

Whatever it was, it had been something very, very bad.

WANT MORE CREEPINESS?
Then you're in luck, because P. J. Night has
some more scares for you and your friends!

THE MIRRORED MESSAGE

Lots of Elizabeth clones came and went before Beth, and they left Beth a coded message to warn her. Can you interpret the previous clones' clue?

Circle the letters in the top half of the mirror that don't match the reversed letters on the bottom. The remaining letters written in order reveal a warning for Beth.

GFJDWSFRFHRDGGJ
FDHGVRGTJDFHSWQ
JHTFTQDDCFLKGYD
OGSPXZAFBYTLHFD
XZVFIAHKLFBJXTA

GFWDWSAFRRDGEJ
FDOGRGTBDFESWO
JHBFTEDDCTLKGHD
TGSOXZEFLYTIHZA
XZBFEAHKLNIJCTE

YOU'RE INVITED TO . . .
CREATE YOUR OWN SCARY STORY!

Do you want to turn your sleepover into a creepover? Telling a spooky story is a great way to set the mood. P. J. Night has written a few sentences to get you started. Fill in the rest of the story and have fun scaring your friends.

You can also collaborate with your friends on this story by taking turns. Have everyone at your sleepover sit in a circle. Pick one person to start. She will add a sentence or two to the story, cover what she wrote with a piece of paper, leaving only the last word or phrase visible, and then pass the story to the next girl. Once everyone has taken a turn, read the scary story you created together aloud!

I live in a pretty normal town with lots of normal buildings, like the mall, the high school, and the pizza place. But there's one building that's not like all the others. It's the old hospital that's been abandoned for sixty years. Most of the windows are cracked or long blown out,

and there are even a few rusty old wheelchairs
on the front lawn. My parents told me never to
go inside the abandoned hospital, but one night
a couple of my friends and I wanted to see just
what was inside. As soon as we walked through
the front doors, we saw . . .

_____

_____

_____

_____

_____

_____

_____

_____

_____

_____

_____

_____

_____

THE END

A lifelong night owl, **P. J. NIGHT** often works furiously into the wee hours of the morning, writing down spooky tales and dreaming up new stories of the supernatural and otherworldly. Although P. J.'s whereabouts are unknown at this time, we suspect the author lives in a drafty, old mansion where the floorboards creak when no one is there and the flickering candlelight creates shadows that creep along the walls. We truly wish we could tell you more, but we've been sworn to keep P. J.'s identity a secret . . . and it's a secret we will take to our graves!

EVERY SECRET LEADS TO ANOTHER

SECRETS
of the MANOR

Hidden passages, mysterious
diaries, and centuries-old secrets
abound in this spellbinding series.
Join generations of girls from
the same family tree as they
uncover the secrets that lurk
within their sumptuous
family manor homes!

EBOOK EDITIONS ALSO AVAILABLE

SecretsoftheManorBooks.com • Published by Simon Spotlight • Kids.SimonandSchuster.com

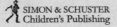